M000252106

ALEX LIDELL

TRIAL OF THREE

POWER OF FIVE BOOK 3

～

SIGN UP FOR NEW RELEASE NOTIFICATIONS at
https://links.alexlidell.com/News

LERA

*T*he air explodes, the magic flowing from my fingers igniting into brilliant flame. The practice arena's sand shoots up toward the blinding sky as tongues of red and orange mate to spawn smoke and sparks.

I stumble backward, my body striking a wall of hard muscle. The scent of pine and citrus washes over me, beating back the bitter tang of ash filling the broiling air. Tye's corded arms wrap around my body, cocooning me in power and safety. For a split second, everything goes silent and still.

And then the magic I threw strikes the ward protecting the top of the arena, the dull *bummm* of impact echoing through my body. A heartbeat seems to stretch on for an eternity . . . before all that debris I so gloriously sent up into the air rains right back down on me. The sand, the rocks, the flames.

I scream, raising my arms to block my face, as if that will do any good. I might be able to echo Tye's magic as if my body were some preternatural mirror, but I certainly can't reflect any of his control of the bloody power.

Tye's arms tighten around me, confident and unyielding. Small pulses ripple through the phantom limb of my magic as Tye nudges it aside, his own power stretching with lazy grace and taking over. An instant later, the falling debris crashes against Tye's shimmering shield, the rocks and sand and fire sliding down obediently to sputter out against the ground.

My heart stutters, my breath coming in hard, sharp bursts, my shoulders pressing shamelessly against Tye. My body, still filled to the brim with the echo of his magic, is somehow awake down to each fiber while feeling like absolute mush. I hadn't realized just how powerful the large, easygoing male truly is, not before now. Echoing Tye's magic is akin to leashing a wild tiger; you've little control over who holds whom. And when that leash snaps . . . I shudder, looking at the five-foot crater in the middle of the practice arena where a candle once stood.

"I . . ." My voice breaks, my mouth dry. I can't bear to turn my head toward where the other members of our quint, River, Coal, and Shade, stand witness to my latest disaster. The ancient magic that made me a weaver, able to echo and weave together the magic of others, unfortunately failed to send an instructional text along. In the week since the second trial announced my ability to the whole Citadel, Autumn has had help from Klarissa herself to cobble together what's known of my power, which is little beyond its theoretical potential. For now, I'm failing gloriously at controlling just one magical cord —one that Tye wields as easily as he breathes—let alone four.

Maybe mastering such magic takes centuries. I have one more week—as far back as River was able to push our retake of the first trial. Stars, but I hate the Citadel's damn rules. Its deadly games. Maybe a weaver was never meant to be a mortal.

Tye's velvety lips brush my ear, reclaiming my attention. My body reacts to the sensual touch involuntarily, blood diverting to the suddenly sensitive juncture of my neck and ear.

"You do like things big, don't you, lass?" Tye whispers.

I—I gasp as Tye's sharp teeth nip the top of my earlobe. The tiny sting races through me, indignation shoving away the fear. My mouth dries, the sensation tingling along my skin. "Bastard," I hiss.

Tye chuckles and slips his hands lower on my waist, resting his large palms comfortably on the crests of my hips. "That's my lass."

"I did technically light the candle," I mutter. After my one and only training session with River, when I felt none of his magic, I expected the chief problem going forward to lie squarely in the "it's not working" camp. Instead, with Tye's fire magic, I'm fortunate if I don't blow up the entire mountaintop. The image of a tiger returns to my thoughts. Adorable when sleeping, apocalyptic when nudged awake.

"Let's try it again, Leralynn," River says, stepping toward Tye and me. The commander's gray eyes are steady, but the hand he runs through his short brown hair betrays his frustration with the absolute lack of progress. Beautiful, hard, and the most closed-off male I've ever met—immortal or otherwise—the prince of Slait is used to elite fae warriors, not twenty-year-old magical strays. Face unreadable, River tosses me another candle from his never-ending stash, the hunk of wax thunking down a foot away from me. "This time, try to light the wick, not the world."

I glare at the candle, a sibling to the ten others I've massacred this afternoon. Not only am I efficiently *not* weaving mystically powerful magical knots, but I think I'm actually

3

getting worse with each repetition. At this rate, next week's trial will probably roast the whole Citadel until it can be served to Mors with a side of potatoes.

"Ready, Lilac Girl?" Tye asks softly.

I rub my eyes with the heels of my hands, holding on to the feeling of Tye's muscular body warming my back. "Has magically lighting a candle ever saved anyone's life?" I ask, keeping my voice low enough for only Tye to hear. Buying a few more seconds to shore up my resolve. "I think it's safe to say that if I need to use your fire magic, it will be for something more spectacular than creating an evening ambience."

"Is waging war the only use you can think of for this new toy?" Tye clicks his tongue, his hands tightening on my hips. "I thought mortals had better imaginations."

"I—" My mouth snaps shut midsentence as tiny prickles of heat suddenly dance along my abdomen, circling my navel. *Prick. Prick. Prick.* The quick, hot touches scatter over my skin, each sizzling prickle igniting my nerves. Teasing my body. My breath catches, the world blinking around me for a heartbeat, then focusing with inappropriate intensity low in my pelvis. "What are you doing?"

"Mmm," Tye drawls lazily, even as his iron grip holds me in place. "I'm . . . educating."

The sparks tour my navel one more time before impudently hopping lower.

My thighs clench together, my skin flushing with enough heat to rival the inferno of moments ago. Certainly enough for Tye to take note. The male bends his head, first his nose and then his velvet lips brushing the inside of my ear. "I do enjoy watching you learn, lass."

4

Prick. Prick. Prick.

I wriggle, which only presses me deeper into Tye's chest. Into a different hardness. Stars.

"The others are watching." My words escape through clenched teeth, my body rising to the provocation even as my mind screams the wrongness of it. Do the other males realize what's happening? Can they *smell* the wetness quickly coating the inside of my thighs? The insistent throbbing that makes standing still impossible? My face blazes. Thank the stars, the uniform's black pants and long, wine-colored tunic have a chance of concealing the visual evidence of my arousal, if not its scent. My thick auburn hair, which started in a neat wreath around the back of my head, now curls against my damp temples and sticks to my forehead. I'm surprised steam isn't rising off my skin where it touches the cool air.

Ice. I make myself think of ice. And slimy sclices. And . . .

Prick. Prick. Prick.

I bite back a scream as Tye's sparks march lower again. When they infiltrate my sex, my heart stops altogether. There is *hair* there. Hair that can catch fire.

A soft, sensual chuckle. "I think you are a little wet to burn, lass," Tye murmurs, as if reading my mind.

"Tye, please." My voice is strangled. Breathless with the focus on one very awake spot, which zings with every beat of my now-galloping heart. With every touch of Tye's prickling magic. I try to shove myself subtly away from his hold and succeed only in dancing in place. Shifting my weight under me, I bite back a whimper. "You've made your point."

"Oh, if it's my *point* you are after, just squirm your backside a bit more, and—"

"Bastard," I gasp, my sex now moist and starting to throb

hard enough to make the world flicker at the edges. My toes curl inside my boots as blazing heat consumes my skin, my face.

A deep chuckle rumbles through Tye's chest, the extra vibrations little helping my cause. "I'm only showing you the versatility of the magic," he drawls. "Since you brought it up."

Suddenly the ground shakes beneath us, knocking Tye and me unceremoniously onto the sand. The sparks wreaking havoc between my legs sputter out against the slick moisture, leaving an ache so intense that I hiss from denied need. Rising onto my hands and knees, I look up to find River striding toward us.

"My apologies," the prince of Slait says, extending his hand with bloody dignified courtesy. "My magic seems to have slipped its leash for a moment."

Tye climbs to his feet, a grin on his face as he shakes his head to rid his red hair of sand. "Happens to the best of us." His emerald eyes and small silver earring catch the sun.

Face flaming, I scramble to my feet, my pulse and breath both racing. My eyes grip the latest of River's candles, my one lifeline out of this mess before one of the males says something that really does make me burst from embarrassment. Candle. Exercise. Magic. Light the candle.

I focus on the power I still feel rumbling from Tye—wicked and strong and gloriously amused. The magic echoes through me as it has all morning, its mischievous tang prickling my tongue like an unripe fruit. I extend my hands toward the candle, the image of a tiny white flame filling my world. I let the power roll from me, a phantom limb following the direction of my hands—

The air crackles with lightning. Missing the candle entirely, the flaming sphere I didn't see forming rushes

6

toward River like a wild beast scenting prey. "Watch out!" I scream.

The commander throws up a hand and the fire I just launched ricochets off his defense and heads right back toward me.

"Shield!" Tye shouts.

I drop to the ground and am still trying to imagine how to weave the power into a barrier when the air before me hardens like glass. River's earthy scent fills my nose as my errant flames slide down the male's second shield and sizzle against the sand.

Cringing, I sit on my heels and force myself to meet the prince's gray eyes. "Thank you."

Before River can answer, a loud, slow clapping sounds from the observation platform above. The practice arena falls silent. River pulls me up to my feet and behind him as Klarissa climbs down the ladder and strides toward us.

"How wonderfully effective." The female's musical alto rings through the arena as Coal and Shade, the latter in his wolf form, come to stand beside Tye, River, and me.

My breath catches. How long was the elder standing there? Watching. Judging. Planning.

"Is this what you call training nowadays, River?" Klarissa's rich lavender gown swishes around her ankles as she turns to the quint commander. Her gleaming dark-brown waves frame a tear-shaped diamond hanging against her forehead like a third eye. Her olive skin looks smooth as porcelain in the sunlight. "One trainee has free rein to do as she wishes? No consequences. No need for correction. If I'd known the effectiveness of this new pedagogy, I'd have brought lemonade and sweet tarts along."

It's a battle to keep myself from stepping back, turning my face to the ground. Not from Klarissa's words themselves—I

7

know better than to expect anything short of well-aimed poison from the viper—but because of how close they hit to the frustration I've seen in River's eyes. It *isn't* working, what we've been doing. I know it. River knows it. And now Klarissa knows it too.

River clasps his hands behind his back. Slow and controlled. His tall, hard body owning every bit of space around him, owning the whole arena without trying. The protectiveness fanning from him surrounds me as potently as Tye's arms did minutes ago. "A pleasure to see you today, Elder. Can we be of assistance?"

Klarissa picks at invisible lint on her sleeve. "I require your aid in protecting Lunos from Mors's Emperor Jawrar. Can I expect your quint to be ready to play its part?"

River's jaw tightens. "We are . . . heading in the proper direction, Elder."

Klarissa smiles, her painted lips parting to show long white canines. "I'm glad to hear it. Shall we test your weaver in the pet pen in the meantime?" Catching my confused frown, the female captures my gaze. Her sharp eyes make my stomach tighten. "The portion of this practice arena that exists in the Gloom is well stocked with a variety of Mors trash that've wandered into our traps. Piranhas, sclices, trakans. I'm surprised your friends have not told you about it; most quints start practicing there as soon as they pass a single trial. A small taste of the real world."

"Klarissa." River's voice is cold and hard enough to sever steel.

She turns to him, her own words no softer. "A weaver should make your quint stronger than any Lunos has ever seen. It takes some doing to turn an advantage into a liability, but I must say, you are managing it with superb efficiency." Shaking her head in disgust, the female turns her back to us.

I swallow, my chest tightening around my ribs. "Klarissa is right," I say softly. "We have to do something about me."

"Yes." River nods. "We have to get you the hell away from here."

2

RIVER

*T*he moment dinner ended, River excused himself and headed toward Klarissa's office in the elders' tower. The female didn't make a habit of inviting herself to a quint's training by happenstance; this afternoon's intrusion was nothing short of a calling card.

Dealing with Klarissa—just one of the many things resting like a hundred-ton boulder on River's shoulders. And yet, as he crossed the crisp grass of the square in the golden light of early evening, a cool, wine-flavored breeze in his face, all River could think about was Leralynn's flushed cheeks, the sweet scent of her arousal drifting across the practice arena as Tye's magic toyed with her. It'd taken everything inside River not to send Tye flying to the other side of the sand. For wasting precious minutes that Leralynn needed to prepare for next week's trial, for taking her survival too lightly. But most of all for distracting River. A hundred problems he needed to be solving, and now all he could think about was what he could do to Leralynn to pull that sweet lilac scent out of her.

"What do you want?" River asked, the corner of his mouth twitching when Klarissa startled. Standing in the doorway of her office, River braced his hand on the doorframe and waited for the female to recover her composure. Few beings could come up on her unawares, but this wasn't River's first time playing the game.

"River." Klarissa rose from behind her oak desk, her voice caressing the air as she smiled at him from under long lashes. "An unexpected pleasure."

It was all River could do to keep from snorting at that. A few centuries ago, he might have said that Klarissa's games kept life interesting. Now, with Leralynn in his life, he simply wanted the scheming female as far from his quint as possible.

"But since you are here," Klarissa continued, plucking a small stack of parchment from the corner of her desk, "perhaps you might assist me. I'd be grateful for a second set of eyes on these reports." She walked around to the sitting area in the corner of her well-appointed office, the expensive brocade chairs, warm lamp, and low glass table providing an illusion of intimacy.

Hands behind his back, River strolled forward and politely accepted the papers. He sank into one of the chairs as he read, his brows drawing together. Neat handwriting that he recognized as a reliable scout's covered the pages, detailing an attack on Karnish, a border village of Blaze Court. A mining community, Karnish had little by way of other resources, but its location—close to Slait and the Citadel—was valuable in its own right. Moreover, if River remembered his geography correctly, Karnish sat on high, strategically advantageous ground.

Klarissa sat prettily across from River, crossing her thighs. "If you wouldn't mind," she said, waving her hand toward a bottle of wine and two glasses that she'd retrieved while River read. She nodded toward the reports. "What do you make of these?"

"The same thing you do, I imagine." River smoothly uncorked the bottle, filled the glasses, and handed one to Klarissa, keeping his face still as stone when she traced her fingers along his. Keeping his voice even was a greater struggle. "It smells of Jawrar attempting to establish a foothold in Blaze, a more blatant precursor to an invasion attempt than we've yet seen." The increasingly thinning wards between Lunos and Mors couldn't stop sclices, much less messages and coins. Not since a few centuries ago, when the Night Guard— Jawrar's Lunos-based sympathizers—had become a legitimate enemy force.

"If Blaze falls, I imagine Slait will be next. *Your* court, River."

"My father's court." Once, uttering such words would have cut River's heart, but there was nothing left there to bleed now.

Klarissa swirled her wine, watching the thick red liquid coat the glass and drip down the sides. "If the Night Guard invades Blaze, it would destabilize all of Lunos. Make it more difficult to protect ourselves against Mors—and Mors *will* come, River. Sooner or later, the qoru will stop using Night Guard proxies and step into Lunos themselves. Blaze is clawing its way free of a drought; it can barely feed its people just now, much less muster an army. If Slait could send troops, head off this attack at the pass—"

River snorted, his lips pressing together into a thin, unamused smile. "If you imagine me to have more sway over King Griorgi now than I did before, I fear you'll be sorely disappointed." River had tried to play his father. *Once.*

Centuries ago, before the quint magic called him. It was how River had first met Klarissa, a council elder even then, one more than happy to feed the young prince of Slait information to aid in running his kingdom. Opening his eyes to the truth. To *her* truth.

For a time, River had even succeeded. With Klarissa's guidance, he'd raised a small army to patrol Slait's Gloom and rallied enough public support for the idea to force the king's hand. His father had been furious about being forced to divert resources from Slait's armies, which could have conquered Blaze for him, into defending against the phantom threat of Mors.

That night, King Griorgi gathered his children in River's bedroom and butchered their mother. To teach River a lesson —and prove his power over his son once and for all. Then the bastard left the bloody body to soak River's mattress. The prince of Slait died with the queen that day. And when the quint call came, River never looked back.

Klarissa set down her goblet and leveled River with her eyes, her sharp gaze sending ice down River's spine. "I think Griorgi is beyond being swayed, River. And that it's time for his son to take the throne of Slait Court. For you and me to join forces against Jawrar."

The wine going down River's throat missed its pipe and he doubled over coughing.

"You cannot run forever," Klarissa said quietly. "Will you at least go to Karnish, see for yourself what may be there? Make your decision based on the facts of today, not centuries past?"

River tapped the runes on his neck—ironically forced there by Klarissa's own scheming—which kept him confined to the Citadel grounds.

The female clicked her tongue. "There is an allowance to leave for the third trial. Call the trial now and I'll ensure you find yourself in Karnish. Really, River, you are sometimes too self-righteous for common sense."

"My answer is no." River rose, his heart beating so hard that he feared the vibration alone would spill the wine. "Politics is not my battlefield. You want to dethrone a king? Find yourself another idiot for the job. As for you and me joining in any way . . ." He stepped closer, ice filling his words. "I will surrender myself to Mors before I do that."

Without waiting for an answer, River turned toward the door.

"You are wrong for that girl, Prince," Klarissa called after him, her voice tinged with pity. River paused without turning around. "And even if you pursue this folly, she is *mortal*. Perhaps that is why the magic chose her—a weaver's power is too great to be in the open for too long. If Leralynn does not perish in battle, she will perish in time. You have responsibilities. To your quint, to Lunos, and to your court. You'll have to stop running from them sometime—and when that time comes, you will need my help."

3

LERA

I frown at the night sky, its brilliant stars glittering sharply outside our suite's windows. Despite the late hour, River has yet to return, and the gnawing in the pit of my stomach grows stronger by the minute—which does little good for my already atrocious card game. Finding Autumn looking in the same direction, her beautiful gray eyes distant, I set the cards down, interrupting the game that Tye, Coal, Autumn, and I have spread across the common room table. Shade's wolf remains curled up beside me on the couch, huffing softly in his sleep. "Worried about him too?" I ask.

"Who?" Legs tucked beneath her in a soft armchair, the petite female absently twists an earring between her thumb and forefinger. The little emerald in a silver setting matches her cropped shirt and flowing pants, which ride low on a taut abdomen. Her silky blond braids are gathered in a knot on top of her head.

I frown. "River. He went to see Klarissa hours ago."

Autumn blinks, her usually sparkling eyes taking a moment to focus. "River? Oh, that one can brood for days, and there are few who set him off more efficiently than Klarissa. Don't expect him back until morning."

Tye chuckles. "I wager it isn't River who Sparkle is thinking about just now, Lilac Girl. And it certainly isn't her cards either."

Autumn narrows her gaze at the green-eyed male, looking for all the world certain that she is the bigger of the pair. "I'd ask what you are talking about, but any glimpse into your thoughts would drive me straight to the baths."

"My thoughts, is it?" Tye grins, his sharp canines flashing. "Tell you what. Wager that earring of yours on the next hand and I'll set *all* my winnings against it."

Autumn's hand drops from her ear, her face turning a shade of red bright enough to get my full attention. Now that I'm looking closely, the little emerald stud does look familiar, conjuring the memory of a different pointed ear. One attached to a tall, attractive warrior with blue eyes, short dark hair, and a wonderful full-souled laugh.

"Kora?" I say, the corners of my mouth lifting. I knew the female quint commander had an interest in my friend—I just hadn't realized that Autumn returned the sentiment. "Since when? And I thought you preferred the dumber of the species."

Tye gives an indignant huff while Autumn aims for nonchalance—and fails. "I like them both. As for Kora, we are just friends."

"Of course. And Tye isn't cheating at cards," Coal says dryly, his eyes a cold blue flame even in the shimmering candlelight.

"You are a graceless loser. It little becomes you, Coal." Tye straightens his silk shirt cuffs—orange, like the fire he wields. I might enjoy being out of uniform in the evenings, but Tye savors fashion almost as much as Autumn does. Figures—the male does nothing by halves. Stretching, he leans back on the couch, one arm slipping around my shoulders to tuck me casually against him.

"I don't imagine Tye would cheat us," I say, feeling the steady beat of the male's heart through his warm, muscled side.

All three of them snort in unison.

"Of course he would," Coal says, his voice as dark as his black leather pants and sleeveless tunic.

"I'd cheat anyone, lass," Tye says, a trace of pity in his voice. "But the three of you are so awful that it's below my dignity. And that says a lot, trust me. At least the flea transport over there is worth cheating."

Shade's wolf lifts his head and bares his teeth at Tye, golden eyes flashing.

My chest warms. Family. These squabbling, brilliant, impudent beings have become my family.

Tye licks my ear.

Shade lunges for him, a flash of gray and black.

Yes, family. Complete with our own village idiots. I grab the scruff of the wolf's neck before he can overturn the card table.

"How long until he can shift back?" I ask Autumn, keeping ahold of the beast until he condescends to accept a belly rub as a consolation prize for not disemboweling Tye. Having damaged his magic in a fruitless attempt to rescue me during the last trial, Shade's recovery is safer in his animal form.

Though I love the wolf, I miss the feel of the fae warrior himself, his warm, golden skin and his velvet voice caressing my ears. We haven't been able to . . . reconnect since that night in the baths over a week ago. Now that I've tasted the real thing, going without is more frustrating than I ever imagined.

"A few more days." The petite female plucks a glass of wine from Tye's hand and takes a sip. "But he shouldn't be using his magic for at least a week. Not if he doesn't want to risk permanent damage."

Permanent damage. My heart tightens, my hand stilling on the soft fur. Me. This is all because of me. My inability to fight, to harness the magic I'm supposed to be controlling. Klarissa wasn't wrong to note the lack of progress in my training, and whatever she's said to River about me tonight . . . Fatigue washes over me and I push myself to my feet. "You lot can continue insulting each other," I say with a lightness I no longer feel. "I'm going to check on Sprite and head to bed." Smoothing down my yellow silk skirt and wide-necked sweater that keeps sliding off one shoulder, I give the room a wave and start toward the suite's door.

"Want company, lass?" Tye calls, his grin widening when the wolf growls again, raises his tail, and demonstratively trots through the door I just opened.

"Goodnight, Tye." I hurry after Shade, my hopes of beating the beast to the stables diminishing with each step. I fully understand why Shade's wolf upsets the horses—what I can't comprehend is why the wolf enjoys it so much. Having seen Czar, Coal's black stallion, nearly crack Shade's ribs for trying to nip his tail, I'm not sure which of the animals I worry about more.

My last hope of finding all well dies when I see that the stable door has been left slightly ajar, giving the wolf just enough room to squeeze through and wreak havoc.

Sighing, I push the door the rest of the way open, inhaling the thick, comforting scent of hay and horses. The long, cavernous space is filled with soft candlelight, thanks to a row of lanterns hanging from the peaked ceiling far above. I've never seen them unlit, but I've also never seen a single stable hand climb up to reignite them. I can only imagine that magic is involved—presumably one that also keeps the lanterns from accidentally falling and setting the barn ablaze. Thick wooden rafters cross overhead, twined with playful strands of shiny green ivy. Long noses dip curiously out of the stall windows, snorting and neighing their welcome, and a small ice chip of tension melts in my chest.

In the largest stall at the far end of the stable, a pair of heavy black hooves tries to take down the barn wall—proof that both Czar and Shade are, in fact, in residence. Reaching into my pocket, I pull out an apple I snagged for Sprite and turn the other way. "There you are, girl," I say, rubbing the mare's soft gray head while she blinks long lashes back at me.

"There you are, cub."

I jump, dropping the apple as Shade's velvet voice echoes through the stable. My heart still racing, I turn to find Shade leaning against one of the stable posts. The male wears loose gray trousers that hang on the crests of his hips—and nothing else. The skin on his hard abdomen is a golden tan that matches his eyes. Black hair hangs in shining waves to his shoulders, the smooth planes of his face shifting in the lantern light. My mouth dries, my breath quickening. Stars, but I've missed that face in the seven days since . . . I swallow. Since

21

ALEX LIDELL

Shade injured himself over *me* so badly that even his wolf wouldn't accept comfort.

Shade's soft steps measure the distance between us, each tap of his foot against the wooden floor injecting a fresh zap of tension into the air. I ache for him so badly that my body refuses to move in fear that he might disappear.

"Throwing apples?" Shade says, picking up the fallen fruit and holding it out to me.

When I reach for it, he pulls the apple up and out of my reach, a corner of his mouth lifting. "Much better," he murmurs. "I'd forgotten just how short you really—"

My toes push me up of their own accord, my head tipping back to meet Shade's lowering mouth. Soft, warm lips cover mine as muscled arms brush my shoulders, my arms, my—

I squeak as Shade tosses the apple into Sprite's stall and grips my hips. Lifting me easily, he brings my face even with his and deepens the kiss. With no ground beneath my feet, I wrap my legs around Shade's hard waist, feeling his low growl all the way through my core.

The smell of earth fresh from rain fills me, soothing the jagged, stinging wounds in my heart. Mate. Shade's wolf is my mate, and the two of us . . . My body folds perfectly into his, alive and fulfilled in a way that only the shifter can offer.

"Shouldn't you be a wolf?" I finally manage to say, pulling away from his lips. "The healing magic—"

Shade closes his mouth over mine again, his eyes flashing with a need that is half-living, half-feral. *Later,* his body seems to scream, and I'm in no shape to argue. Especially not when he opens the empty stall beside Sprite and lays me down on the soft, clean straw. His hands caress me, deft fingers pulling away my clothing until I'm dressed only in Shade's desire. And my own.

As I reach down to relieve Shade of his pants, I feel the slickness between my thighs already coating my skin. The hard bulge under Shade's trousers says the male is ready for me as well—so ready that a shiver racks his body at the merest brush of my fingers along his hard, throbbing shaft.

4

LERA

*W*hen I push Shade onto his back for a better look, I find his cock somehow even larger than I remembered. Erect. Throbbing. Dressed in a bead of enticing moisture, the sight of which sends a zing of want right down to my sex. Stars. Reaching out, I brush the cock's velvety underside.

Shade whimpers.

A wicked delight blooms inside me, fueled by the memory of a certain male who made me beg in a certain bathing room.

"Cub—" Shade's eyes widen as he sees my grin, but my hands are already gripping the bare crests of his hips, my gaze teasing his twitching cock.

Bringing my mouth a hair's breadth from the head, I blow gently over his skin, starting with ruffling the curly tufts of coarse black hair and ending squarely on the tip of my target. Then, with no warning, I flick my tongue and lap that thick, salty droplet right off.

Shade jerks, his strangled whine so wolfish that my heart

speeds with feral excitement. The thrill of taking him into my mouth, of tasting him, fills me to the brim.

I lick him again, this time caressing his cock all the way along its glorious length, feeling the thick vessels hugging its underside, luscious and firm beneath my tongue. I pull away, replacing my tongue with my hands and rubbing the shaft only long enough to tease a breath from him. And then . . . then I take the whole of him into my mouth, suckling greedily.

Shade's body shakes with a tension I recognize all too well from when he once did this to me. Each of his noises, his flinches of pleasure, fuels my own need.

"You . . . are . . . evil," Shade manages to say, his hands curling in my hair and shaking as much as the rest of him.

I stop, find his yellow eyes, glazed with strain, and hold them as I take him deeper. Withdraw. Nip the sensitive underside of his cock, just below the head.

That, I discover a moment later, proves a strategic mistake.

With a roar of need, Shade yanks me up, tossing me onto my belly atop a quickly recruited flake of hay. I gasp at the feeling of my backside suddenly in the air, my sex raised for the taking. All thought leaves with the next breath as Shade settles on top of me, his knees spreading my wet thighs. Gripping my hips, the male sheathes himself inside me with a single, glorious thrust. His thickness fills a void inside me so thoroughly that when his hand comes around to stroke my bud, my whole body already hangs on the cliff's edge.

The same edge that Shade rides himself.

We move together, again, again, holding on for the last heartbeats of unbearable strain. Then Shade's lips find my ear, his voice raw. "I love you, mate," he growls, sending us both tumbling off the cliff into an abyss of pleasure and agony and stars.

I find no words to utter in the wake of release, but none need be said. Shade pulls me up and settles me into the hollow of his shoulder, the thin sheen of sweat on his skin carrying his wonderful male musk.

The utter joy of our connection is as warm as a blanket, as warm as the male wrapping me in his arms. As I close my eyes, content in Shade's strength, I wonder if the wolf's mating bond hasn't seeped into me as well.

I WAKE to the infant rays of a chilly dawn piercing my eyes. For a moment, as memories of last night wash over me, twin fires of pleasure and guilt kindle in my chest. The latter, a condition of encouraging Shade's shift from wolf form, sputters out as quickly as it came.

Having wisely shifted back before returning from the stable, Shade's wolf has somehow evicted me not only to a scrap of mattress but to the worst scrap of the lot. Trying to pull the blanket over my head to ward off the rays, I discover that this too has been coveted by the two-hundred-pound lump of lupine insolence.

My skin prickling with scratches from tumbling in straw and hay, I prod the beast with my foot. Judging from the sky's soft red cast, I still have a good hour before I need to rise—and I want to spend it in comfort.

Shade's ear twitches, the only sign he gives of being anything but a plush toy. He certainly does not condescend to open his eyes or—stars forbid—*move*.

"Canine parasite." I jab his rump harder with my foot. "If you don't move over, I'm going into Tye's room."

One yellow eye opens, blinking at me unhappily. With a

slowness to match growing grass, the wolf climbs to his feet and lazily stretches his back paws. Then his front paws. Then his back, arching it up, up, up like a cat, then down, raising his tail toward the ceiling. Then—

"Shade!"

Giving me a long-suffering sigh, the wolf takes two steps away from the center of the bed before falling over on his side like a log.

Accepting the compromise, I settle into the newly vacated space. Small but warm and smelling wonderfully of fur and forest. Shade's wolf shuffles himself, curling perfectly against my back, the rhythmic rise and fall of his chest soothing my thoughts. That is, until I feel something prickling my skin and brush the sheet to discover . . . "You're shedding?" I rub stray bits of gray fur off my skin and accept that all hopes of sleep are now gone.

I slip onto the floor, its stone cool and pleasantly rough beneath my bare soles, and take the few steps over to my dresser to pull free a uniform. Loose black breeches, a wine-colored tunic with a wide-open collar—the tailor still not having gotten around to taking in any of the shirts, even the smallest of which are too big on my small frame—and soft leather boots. I take extra care in wrapping a wide sash around my middle, the small touch transforming the uniform into a reasonably tasteful ensemble. I almost toss my nightshirt onto the bed, then remember Shade's fur and think better of it. Of all the countless hazards I'd imagined of bonding with four elite fae warriors, dealing with shedding was somehow never one of them.

When I start the search for my hairbrush, Shade hops down from the bed and out the window, his body a streak of gray fur.

"What—?" I start to say, cutting off with a curse as I finally find my brush.

On the floor. Its once gorgeously carved wooden handle now a tangle of splinters and teeth marks.

DESPITE THE EARLY HOUR, River and Autumn are already in the common room, the male's large body dominating the space without effort. Even sitting behind a worktable, his sleeves rolled up to reveal powerful, corded forearms, River's simple movements as he turns sheets of paper are an exercise in control. When he lifts his gray eyes to me, my bones soften in spite of themselves.

"Leralynn." River rises, the wide sash around his middle tightening against chiseled muscles. "Good morning."

My name in River's low voice echoes through me. Stupid. I'm stupid to let the male get under my skin. To harp on a simple kiss. To want him when he has other things on his mind. When we both do.

"It's good to have you back." I take a step toward him and kiss his cheek, feeling his body go rigid at the touch of my lips. "What did Klarissa want yesterday?"

"Aside from discussing our upcoming trial, nothing of consequence." River pulls a chair out for me across the table, his clean, earthy scent wafting off him.

Putting my hand on the chair's back, I meet River's gaze. *Tell me. Let me in.*

The smooth angles of his face don't budge, his set jaw giving me nothing.

I try not to let the hurt spiraling through me make it to my face.

"Good morning, Lera," Autumn calls from the couch, balancing a book in one hand and chocolate pastry in the other. The female's myriad silver-blond braids cascade down her delicate shoulders, one of which is bare beneath a wide-necked purple top that skims her bellybutton. "There is coffee if you hurry, before the rest of the vultures descend upon it." She points to a tray on the side table, laden with coffee, tea, sweet breads, and fruit. The rich, bitter smell of roasted beans fills my nose as I pour the hot liquid into a delicate painted cup.

"I fear Autumn has already laid claim to the chocolate bread," River says, passing a scone to me. "I was smart enough not to argue."

"See, so you *can* be reasonable, rare as the occasion is," Autumn says. "Speaking of reasonable, Klarissa told Kora last night that her quint is ready for the third trial. Which is horseshit."

Returning to his seat, River takes a sip of coffee, setting the cup down carefully to avoid the documents. "If Klarissa says the quint is ready, I imagine they are." His gaze returns to his reading. "The female is practical to a fault. As I see no reason why she might wish Kora's quint dead, her decree of readiness is likely genuine."

"I don't like 'likely,'" Autumn says, her body tight.

River turns over a page. "Liking it is not a requirement."

I frown at the male. Being a jerk to me is one thing. Adding Autumn into the mix is unacceptable.

"What are you reading?" I ask, laying my palm flat over his damn papers. "And don't you dare answer 'nothing of consequence.'"

River looks from my hand to me and lifts a questioning brow. "A report from the council." He waves at the text, his

words calm. Conversational. "You are welcome to read for yourself, Leralynn. In short, the Night Guard attacked a mining village on Blaze Court's northern border. Witnesses now claim to have seen a qoru in the mix."

"Witnesses." Autumn wrinkles her nose. "They probably saw dark hounds and jumped to bards' tales. If the qoru found an open corridor from Mors to Lunos, I don't imagine they'd waste the passage on raiding a few miners." Her brows pull together, that keen intelligence sparkling in her eyes. "Though if Klarissa wanted to get *your* attention, River, the mention of a qoru or two would not go amiss."

"Agreed." River's jaw tightens, something hidden and grim settling over his shoulders. A layer to this news that he refuses to share. "I'll speak to her."

"I'll come with you," I say, careful not to phrase it as a question. River may be the commander of this quint, but I'm not about to stop fighting for him. For us. Catching his gaze, I hold it tightly, raising my chin. My heart quickens. "When you go to meet with Klarissa, I'm going with you."

"No need." Breaking the gaze, River takes another sip of coffee. "Train. Your magic—your weaving—is the priority until both of the remaining trials are behind us. Shade's magic is still recovering, so go with Coal."

Heat rises to my face, the fire inside me growing to match River's ice. "I wish to come with you." My voice is even. Hard. "I will somehow endeavor not to distract the adults."

Autumn snorts.

"I don't want *me* distracting *you*," River says, eyes flashing. "You can involve yourself in politics and strategy *after* you master your powers. Learning control is a better use of your time than listening to me explain all the nuances of these

31

reports—without which the conversation with Klarissa would make little sense to you."

Go play with Coal while the grownups talk. "If training my magic is so important, how come we've not attempted to work with your earth affinity?" I ask sweetly. "Not since before we even knew me to be a weaver."

River runs a hand through his hair. A tell. The prince is worried. About me? The reports? Something else? My body tightens, the not knowing like a scrape of nails on stone.

"You cannot catch up on three centuries of political intrigue in three weeks, Leralynn," he says finally. No apology, not even a hint of one, shining behind his gray eyes. "We all have our duties. Just now, yours is to harness magic and mine is to confer with Klarissa on these reports she sent me."

My blood sizzles. "And if I insist, *Prince*?"

Reaching across the table, River takes hold of my chin, his grip tightening when I attempt to jerk free. "Then I will order you to stand down, Leralynn," he says without blinking an eye. "And you will obey."

5

LERA

I walk with Coal to the sparring ring in silence, barely noticing the gleaming white buildings and flowering vines, the manicured lawns and bustle of scholars and warriors going about their business. In my own way, I've become used to the Citadel—its toxic sweetness and echoing grandness.

The conversation with River still burns in my chest, making bile crawl up my throat. It's good that it's Coal working with me today. Good that in a few minutes I'll be knocked about so hard, I won't have time to fume over River's orders. Good that I'll have somebody I can try to kill.

"I heard," Coal says, his voice a low rumble.

"Heard what?" I focus on the sand in front of us, raked smooth by the Citadel's invisible servants, the fence around it showing a fresh coat of white paint.

The warrior taps his pointed ear. "Your argument with River. Everyone in the suite did."

Damn fae and their bloody hearing. And here I thought it

was the early hour that kept the other males out of the common room. Fine. It wasn't a secret. "River is a bastard."

"Yes." Coal vaults over the fence while I opt for the gate. "But he's also right."

My jaw tightens but I keep my thoughts to myself. I'm not going to discuss River with Coal, not when I can't discuss *Coal* with Coal. The male saved my life back in the trial arena, plunging himself into his own nightmares until they overwhelmed him. Forcing his strange magic to lash out in agony and bridge the gap between us.

It was Coal's power flowing through my veins, my muscles, my heart, that let me fight off Malikai. And yet when the fight ended . . . Coal said nothing of it. Not when I asked. Not when I woke drenched in sweat, the echoes of Coal's nightmares shaking my body. Certainly not when those nightmares flickered in *his* blue eyes, turning them a shade of purple.

All my males have sacrificed so much for my sake— surrendering their dignity to wear the runes of Citadel initiates, suffering echoes of hell to grant me magic, offering their lives for mine—but discussing it? That's a bridge too far.

Pulling off the wide sash holding the uniform tunic against his body, Coal hangs the cloth on the waist-high rail. A moment later, he grabs the back of his shirt with thickly corded arms, drawing it over his head without disturbing a single hair in his tight blond bun. My mouth dries, my hands suddenly longing to touch Coal in a way that has nothing to do with combat. His bare torso is smooth and defined enough to make a sculptor jealous, the hard pectorals mirroring the carved squares of his abdomen. A thin pink line snakes around the curve of his left shoulder, the fading footprint of a whip's tail that must have wrapped itself around his flesh last week. I know the view from the back is far worse, last week's lashings joining a crisscrossed pattern of old scars from his days in Mors, nearly covering up the odd tattoo twining down his spine.

My jaw tightens. As he dismissed my request this morning, River didn't fight against Coal's punishment either, not even when I begged the prince to keep Coal away from the whipping post. A commander and his underlings. Seeing that pink line on Coal's skin, I realize just how sick of River's attitude I'm getting.

Coal's piercing blue gaze follows the path of mine and hardens. "Stop worrying about my flesh and start worrying for your own."

Well, at least he didn't guess the other reason I was gazing at his chest. Grabbing a practice sword off a rack, the male tosses it into my hands before selecting another weapon for himself. He swings the sword in a wide, lazy circle, even that casual movement a study in precision. "Speaking of which, Shade's healing magic is still recovering, so whatever marks you collect this morning are yours to keep."

I twirl the wood, getting used to its weight. A month ago I'd never even held a weapon, and now the blade greets me like—well, it would be a lie to call it a *friend*, but perhaps an acquaintance. A translator. If normal beings use words and phrases to communicate, Coal prefers blows and parries. I tie my unruly auburn hair back into a knot and bring the practice blade to ready guard. "Save your breath, Coal. I've not been afraid of you for some time."

Coal's eyes darken, flecks of purple flashing through the brilliant blue. "That is a mistake, mortal." His low voice sends a shiver down my spine. Before I can respond—before I can think—the male swings his blade into my sword arm.

35

I hear the strike before I feel it, a limb-numbing pain that explodes inside my flesh. I swallow a shout, only the threat of a repeat blow keeping my weapon in my hand. Bastard. Bloody sadistic bastard. Every thought of caressing Coal's velvet muscles goes out of my mind in an instant. Blood simmers in my veins, pulsing through my newly forming welt. Through my head. My world narrows to Coal.

His blade circles back, his muscles rippling beneath bare skin. The weapon twirls smartly in the air and snaps for my skull.

Planting my foot in the sand, I thrust my blade up to parry the blow. The wooden swords meet deafeningly above my head, making my teeth clank together as my arms buckle beneath the strain. That attack—it too was harder than it needed to be.

"What the hell are you doing?" I gasp, stepping away from the clash just before Coal's sword smashes through both my defense and my head. "Are you insane?"

"Insane?" Coal parrots, aiming for my knees. When I jump away to save myself from a shattered joint, the tip of his blade cruelly clips my shoulder. "Insane is a weaver playing with magic instead of controlling it. Insane is a mortal challenging the quint's commander. Insane"—Coal circles me, his sword slicing a pattern of deadly blows—"is training the same way and expecting a different result."

I open my mouth but shut it again without speaking, the need to protect my head outweighing all thought.

"Klarissa was right yesterday." Coal spits the words, his muscles moving in smooth, deadly arcs. *Clank. Clank. Clank.* His eyes are dark. Merciless. "What we've been doing is child's play that does no one any good. And I, for one, am done playing."

I say nothing. I've no breath to waste on such frivolities.

Coal's attack takes on a pattern, each blow making up in power for what it lacks in uniqueness. Low, middle, high. Low, middle, high. *Clank, clank, clank.*

My breath hitches, my muscles burning as I struggle to keep up with the dance. Each parry, each step, a desperate bid to forestall the inevitable impact. Sweat soaks my hair and drips down to sting my eyes, my boots' purchase on the sand more precarious with each lunge. I sidestep, bringing my sword up to block a high blow that I can't even see but guess is coming.

A harsh pain blossoms across my ribs instead. I gasp, the futility of it all cinching like a noose around my throat. Stars, Coal hasn't done this to me since that first training day in the mortal world. My foot slips and I fall to one knee.

The warrior doesn't even slow down.

Our blades crack above my head, pressing against each other. My lungs burn, my arms shaking with the effort of staving off his blade. "Stop it!"

Coal kicks me, his foot sinking deep into my solar plexus.

I fall back so hard that the world winks. The sword flies from my hand. With the next heartbeat, the male is atop me, his powerful thighs straddling my ribs, his weight an immovable stone atop my chest.

"Better?" Coal demands, showing me his teeth.

I buck, grasping mentally for my training, some part of me still aware that bridging to create space is my only route of escape. Except I can't. Can't lift my hips from the sand. Can't shift Coal's weight off me. Can't move the wrists Coal now has pinned.

The world darkens around its edges until nothing but Coal's perfect, chiseled face fills my sight. My pulse pounds as the male leans down, suffocatingly close. Stealing what little air remains to pull into my lungs. Coal's metallic musk chokes me, his hands on my wrists so tight that my fingers go numb.

"Stop." I mean to shout the word, but it comes out as a mere puff of air. My eyes sting, my body screams at its restraints. I long to go limp, to stop fighting in hopes that darkness might claim me, stopping the torment. Except I can't even do that, for the promise Coal once extracted from me. *Never stop fighting.*

The male forces my wrists together above my head, transferring his hold until one of his large hands traps both of mine. Lifting off me for the briefest of moments, Coal forces me face-down on the sand. Just like . . .

Just like I was in the trial. The fight with Malikai.

Nausea and panic race through me as I follow the realization to its terrifying conclusion. If Coal is recreating my trial fight, then we are in act two of that horrid play. And the final act, the one still to come, is me drawing on Coal's magic to save my life.

I twist my head, desperately searching out his face. My blood chills when I find it. Coal's skin is ashen, his eyes a deep purple-blue, haunted with nightmares. I might be on the sand just now, flopping like a dying fish, but Coal—he is in a Mors dungeon, chained and tormented for the qoru's amusement.

"Stop, Coal," I scream. A demand this time, not a plea. "Stop. Now. For both our sakes."

"Make me." Coal pokes my ribs hard, each jab shooting bolts of pain through my body. "Fight back, mortal. With everything you have." Coal gasps. "Fight with everything *I* have."

The sound of Coal's strangled gasp shatters something inside me, and like hawks flying through an open window, images invade my mind. A cold, gray room. Restraints. The smell of blood and pain that I know are Coal's. A heartbeat later, power flows into me, spreading through my body. Waking it.

I twist with all my might, breaking my tormentor's iron grip. Strength and fury pulse through my veins, dark and corrosive and determined to survive, even if the world cracks for it. I rear back, head-butting the male. Throwing him off me. Air and freedom brush my skin, and I twist about, ready to kill.

I am not ready, however, to find Coal on the ground two paces away, his nose dripping blood to the sand. I've . . . *thrown* Coal. Not just shaken him off, but forced him up and into the air. My magic—Coal's magic—courses through me as I stalk toward the warrior.

The male brings up his hands, already finding his footing, ready to take whatever I throw at him. There is no smile on his face though. No spark of triumph, which I'm sure I'd feel if I wasn't so damn furious.

Yes, it worked. Except that the magic burning inside me is still fueled by the nightmares shredding Coal's soul.

"This was your damn plan?" I shout.

"You needed to echo my magic." Coal's words are labored, as if speaking each one is a battle. "Your staying alive is not negotiable. Not a matter of convenience."

I punch him.

He shifts right and my blow meets nothing but air, his three centuries of combat training making themselves known. Swiping the practice blades off the ground, he tosses one to me. "If you're still worried about me, mortal," he pants, "then I've not worked you hard enough. As for what I do in my head—"

"Torture," I say bluntly, throwing the damn practice blade across the ring. "I believe the word you are looking for is torture. And there is no bloody world in which breaking you apart is an acceptable way of granting me access to your magic." Without waiting for Coal's answer, I dust myself off and leave the sparring ring.

When I glance back, Coal is on his knees, his lean, muscular body shaking like a newborn kitten's.

6

RIVER

*R*iver stared at the door closing behind Leralynn and Coal, counted to sixty, then stalked out into the fresh air. Hooking around to the back of the dormitories, where a wall of lush greenery hid a neck-breaking drop down the mountainside, River found the thin trail that led to the edge of the overlook. Hidden songbirds trilled in every direction and the scents of fresh sap and moist earth filled the air. The dense foliage whipped at River's skin as he walked. He knew he should be more careful, blading his body or at the very least bringing up his hands to ward off the predatory branches, but he couldn't make himself care.

River had done the right thing. Was doing the right thing. However wrong it felt.

It was pitiful, really. He was over five hundred years old, the prince of Slait, the commander of one of Lunos's most powerful quints. And yet when it came to Leralynn, he might as well be a colt. River's hand tightened into a fist. He couldn't free his mind of the female, her fire-filled chocolate eyes as she stormed out of the suite still sending shockwaves of desire through him. Her long lashes, her dusting of rebellious freckles, the curves of her hips and breasts—they were a force of nature. Of magic. Of whatever it was that drove River's self-control to the very cusp. And beneath it all was a spirit that echoed his own. Even when they argued.

Especially when they argued.

It had never been thus with Daz, River realized. Sweet, gentle Daz had never challenged him, not until she walked out of his life. And even then, there was no confrontation, no battle of spirits. She simply . . . left. And River could fight it no more than he could fight the wind.

Leralynn was different. Infuriatingly, wonderfully, frustratingly different. Daz had needed River to protect her from the world. Leralynn needed him to protect her from her own too-brave self. Stars, the female's track record still chilled River's blood. Yes, of course she would trick the whole quint into a connection. Of course she'd agree to the council's terms without a moment's thought. Of course she'd go along with Malikai's idea to spring a second trial. Because why wouldn't a twenty-year-old mortal female name herself a one-person defense force for four elite fae warriors?

If Leralynn caught a whiff of Klarissa's latest scheme to "protect Lunos from Jawrar," there was no telling what the mortal would pull down on the elder's head. And if she heard the notion of River diving into politics or dethroning King Griorgi? Stars. The girl had turned frigid upon discovering River to be a prince . . . What would she think about a plot to seize the bloody throne, even if it wasn't River's idea or desire? More importantly, what would Griorgi do to Leralynn if *he* heard Klarissa's rumblings?

Klarissa. The damn female turned manipulation into an

art form. River might have been a naive colt when he first fell for Klarissa's wit, but the elder had known exactly the stakes of the tune she made him dance to. And when River learned the depths of the monster sitting on Slait's throne—when River's mother paid the price for his insubordination, right in front of his own eyes—Klarissa had been so utterly unsurprised that River wondered if she hadn't calculated it all out before starting the game. She couldn't have known exactly what Griorgi would do, but she knew the king would show his true stripes to River eventually.

Now Klarissa had new plans, except this time, River would ensure that the people he cared for were nowhere near the elder's chessboard.

Pushing past the final curtain of branches, River stepped onto the small, clear lip of the cliff's edge. The wind whipped his short hair, stinging his eyes as he stared out over the vast carpet of treetops, the sparkling reflections of sunlight playing over the river below. A peregrine falcon rode an updraft far out over the valley, hunting for prey with eyes nearly as sharp as River's.

The neutral lands. Breathtakingly beautiful when observed from the Citadel's great height. Deadly when traveled on foot.

Something smacked the back of River's head, bouncing off his skull to the ground. A pinecone. Cocking his foot, River kicked the small woodsy offering right off the cliff.

A second cone hit him a heartbeat later. A third.

River turned, his jaw tightening at the sight of Autumn swinging down from a low-riding tree branch, three more pinecones industriously tucked into her waistband.

"Coward," she said, landing lightly on the ground, her chin pointing into the air.

43

Shifting his weight, River spread his shoulders and glared at his sister in a way that made most warriors blanch.

Autumn snorted. "So you don't deny it?"

"Deny what?"

Toeing off her slippers, Autumn sat on the cliff's edge, her feet dangling over the abyss. "What I said. About you being a coward."

"It took me a few hundred years, but I've officially reached the conclusion that ignoring you is more efficient than arguing. So no, I don't deny anything you say. Could you go bother someone else now? I have a meeting to prepare for."

"Is there a reason you wished to piss off Lera, or were you just bored? Because in case you failed to notice, that didn't go very well." Autumn twisted back to capture River's gaze with her pity-filled one. "Stars, River. You've fallen so hard, you no longer know where your foot and your mouth even are, haven't you?"

River's face heated, a growl that only Autumn could so efficiently draw from him rising through his chest. The little female had no business—

He cut the thought short. If Autumn waited until it was her business to do something, she would not be Autumn. Except River didn't think he could have *two* such females in his life. "She . . . she won't obey me."

"I can hardly imagine anything worse," Autumn said. "How do you even manage to live in the same suite as her, knowing that?"

"This isn't a jest." River pinched the bridge of his nose. "The girl nearly *died* a week ago. Twice. Normal beings would take the time to shake a bit, to recoil from what happened, perhaps delay trying to stride into their would-be murderer's office. Leralynn, on the other hand, seems to be declaring a bloody war on death." It made River simultaneously want to throttle the female and bury himself inside her.

Lowering himself beside Autumn, River plucked one of the pinecones from her waistband and tossed it into the world's vastness. "She is going to get herself killed, Autumn." He'd meant his voice to sound objective, but the damned words tumbled from him in a whisper. The need to protect Leralynn, to wrap her in his arms and shield her from danger, racked River's body so strongly that he wondered how his spine didn't snap from the strain. Just the thought of her lilac scent made his head swim. "She has more courage than experience, more magic than control. If I can't keep her safe . . ." River shook his head, resting his forearms on his knees. "I have to get her away from here. Away from Klarissa."

"Before Klarissa tells her that only help from Slait can keep Jawrar's Night Guard from invading Blaze?" Autumn supplied in that ruthless way she had of slicing to the bone. "And that unless you seize Slait's throne, such help will never come?"

"The council can send fully ordained quints to bulk up Blaze's border. Klarissa *wants* Slait's army; she doesn't *need* it."

Autumn toyed with the tips of her braids. "There are only so many quints. The Citadel was never meant to protect the courts, just the neutral lands between." She held up a hand, warding off River's retort. "The point isn't how or whether the council should interfere in defending Blaze. The point is that you'd rather face Emperor Jawrar himself than go anywhere near Slait's throne, and Leralynn deserves to know that. And the reason why."

A pinecone that River hadn't realized he'd picked up now broke in his hand. Autumn knew all the tiniest imperfections of his soul, and she aimed for each weakness with an archer's precision. It made him want to shove her off the bloody cliff. "And she will," he said. "When the time is right, not when bloody Klarissa decides to play us like dancing string puppets." He shook his head. "Klarissa doesn't care about protecting Karnish as much as she cares about lighting a fire under me to go against King Griorgi. As she has always wanted. Tugging heartstrings to drum up motivation is a damn old trick, and I'm not letting her play it on Leralynn." He paused, finding Autumn's eyes, his mouth suddenly dry with the need to hear his little sister's approval. "Now do you see why I need Leralynn to pass the trials and get the hell out of here?"

"Don't take my head off," Autumn said finally. "But would putting you on Slait's throne be such a bad thing?"

Ice and fire rushed through River's blood, bringing him to his feet. He opened his mouth to tell his sister exactly what she could do with that notion, but it wasn't even worth the breath it would take. "Yes, it would," he said coldly, turning on his heels back toward the dormitories. "And Autumn, Leralynn's life depends on obeying my orders, not on liking me. Interfere, and it will be the last time you and I speak."

7

LERA

"*A*re you limping, Lilac Girl?" Tye inquires, watching me suspiciously as I navigate my plate from the meat and fruit platters toward the table that the males commandeered for the midday meal. After this morning's argument with River, and Coal's idiotic training notion, I'd have refused to share a meal with them altogether except that Kora and her quint are leaving for their third trial after this and the gathering is a bit of a sendoff.

Not that I have a prayer of being good company with the image of Coal's shaking body haunting my every breath, the wrongness of our connection this morning like a layer of vile grease smearing my soul. There has to be a better way. Certainly, there's no further to go in the other direction.

"Lass?" Tye prompts.

I set my plate of watermelon and grilled lamb on the table, pretending to hold the dish with both hands. In reality, my right arm throbs from Coal's opening volley and can't hold a pen, much less a plate. As for limping . . . I frown at my leg. I might be. With all the other parts of my body screaming their displeasure, it's hard to tell what I'm favoring when. My stomach turns at the sight of food. "I'm just hungry."

"Oh, aye," Tye says slowly. "That explains it. Of course."

The dining hall is its usual echoing din, the voices of hungry warriors bouncing off the peaked ceiling two stories above. As always, the occasional head swivels toward me for a quick look, curious about the tiny mortal training alongside the most formidable quint ever to come out of this place. I've grown reasonably good at ignoring it. Thankfully, Malikai and his quint are now keeping their distance, content to glare silently from the far side of the hall.

I glance toward Coal and find the warrior coldly unwilling to meet my eyes, so I choose a seat beside Shade instead. The shifter, in his fae form for the occasion—over Autumn's loud objections—gives me a too-worried look.

I quickly turn to Kora, conjuring a smile. "So, how are you feeling?"

The tall female smiles a bit shyly, so at odds with her usual commanding aura. "Rather excited, to be honest. The runes will allow up to three days to complete the trial, but the council elders told me they expect us back in one, which is encouraging."

Autumn's jaw tightens. "Promise me you'll go for safety over glory, Kora."

Kora's cheeks flush a light pink, her long fingers brushing Autumn's in the first open display of affection I've seen between them. "We will share the evening meal tomorrow. How about I promise you that?"

While Kora wears her quint's usual green tunic, her short brown hair neat and no-nonsense, Autumn looks like she's dressed up for the occasion—or dressed up for Kora. In a silvery green skirt that nips in at her waist and swishes around her legs like water and a matching bandeau top that highlights every inch of her delicate curves, she looks even more like a mischievous wood imp than usual. Her long blond braids are swept back in a high ponytail, showing off the stunning silver hoops shimmering at her ears.

Seeing Autumn's gaze fatally caught on Kora's hand, I take up the reins of the conversation. "Tell me more about the third trial," I say, making my voice light. Festive. "I know the quint is separated and must reunite and find its way back. Is there more to it?"

"I imagine Prince River would be better to ask than I," Kora says, clearly unaware of just how little I want to ask *Prince River* about the latrines, much less the trials.

"That is the essence of it," River says smoothly, his voice betraying nothing of our morning argument. Perhaps it was a nonevent to him. My chest tightens. Coal, Tye, and Shade accept the quint's hierarchy without question, and River appears to expect the same of me. Just another subordinate for a male used to having a whole court bend a knee. River turns slightly, encompassing both Kora and me with his words while the rest of Kora's quint leans in to listen.

I shift my gaze to him, quietly hoping the male will drop a juicy piece of lamb right onto his crisply tailored navy-blue tunic.

"The Field Trial simulates capture and escape," River says. "An elder will blindfold you and take you through the Gloom to your 'capture' location, triggering a rune to make you sleep before he leaves. You will be out for under a minute but it will feel longer when you wake. You will be disoriented. As if you'd truly been captured. Your priority will be to find each other, orient yourselves, and return to the Citadel—likely by finding folds in the Gloom to speed your travel. I recommend that, before the trial, you decide whether your meeting point will be in the Light or the Gloom. And while you don't know the landscape of your trial, you could name a relative meeting spot. The base of the tallest tree in sight, for example. Alternatively, if you have a shifter with an appropriate form, you could agree for everyone to stay put while the animal rounds up the group."

"Celia shifts to a hawk," Kora says, nodding to a dark-haired warrior whose long nose makes me think of a bird's beak. "We plan to gather where the hawk can find us. The Gloom first, and then, if after twelve hours anyone is still alone, we will move into the Light. It will change the distances but create a new avenue of approach."

River nods approvingly and moves on to a discussion of marker placement and strategy that I tune out. The third trial is a ways off for us—anything beyond next week's test is—and for the moment, I've more than enough to occupy my mind.

Including Shade's hand, which I realize has been stroking my hair for some time now.

"Hello, cub," the male purrs, his high cheekbones and full lips only inches from me when I turn to face him. "And here I thought I might need to bite you before you'd grant me attention."

"By the smell of ye, Shade," Tye drawls, "you've had plenty of the lass's attention."

My cheeks flame but Shade's beautiful face only settles into a contented smile as he draws me closer to him. "By the smell of you, you haven't."

I push Shade away, wondering if embarrassment could, in fact, be fatal. "Could you two stop smelling me? And each other? And, just, stop smelling."

A corner of Shade's mouth twitches. "How will we know anything about you if we do that?"

"You could ask."

"Oh, aye," Tye says, rolling his eyes. "Because that worked out well when I asked after your limp a wee bit ago."

Shade's gaze narrows on me, the predatory intent so potent that my heart skips a beat, then quickens in warning. Before I can take defensive measures, he snakes an arm beneath my knees and—ignoring my gasp—lifts me onto his lap.

A low, velvet chuckle brushes the back of my neck as Shade settles me possessively against him. The heat of his large body wraps around me like a blanket, his arms encircling my shoulders and rubbing with heartbreaking gentleness along my bruised and sore flesh. Not healing magic, but a power of a different sort seeps through me, filling me with the male's warmth. "How *did* training go, cub?"

My hand tightens on my fork and I strategically bite into a cube of watermelon, buying a few seconds to conjure an answer. Or better yet, to shove Coal into explaining exactly how flaying himself open was the new prize training strategy.

"It went fine," Coal says finally, slicing through the thickening silence. In his usual sleeveless black tunic and matching pants, the warrior wraps darkness around himself so tightly that there is no telling where one ends and the other begins.

I glare at him.

Coal raises his chin, challenging me to say anything different. Under his skin, lean muscles shift in movements so familiar that it's all I can do to evict the sudden memory of his bare, sweat-slicked torso from my thoughts.

Tye takes a long swig of wine. "Well, Coal is a perpetual optimist, so there is that to consider."

Coal drains his wine cup, nothing of what truly happened visible in his eyes. Centuries of experience concealing the truth, even from his quint brothers, pays its dividends in his steady gaze and confident posture. "Right elbow, lower left ribs, left thigh just above the knee," he says, jerking his chin at me while looking at Shade. "I realize magic isn't an option, but if you've salve, use it."

My mouth opens. With my body one giant ache, Coal's accounting is keener than my own would have been. I left him alone and shaking on the sand, while he kept tabs on my bruises. Stars. Before Coal spoke, I doubted the male had been aware of even landing the strikes, much less which of them left the deepest marks.

Coal catches my gaze. "I choose my targets, mortal. And I hit what I aim for." He rises, his plate now empty. "A skill you'd do well to improve upon before next week." Turning to the table, Coal gives a nod to Kora—his equivalent of a salute for luck—and strides out of the dining hall.

My HANDS ARE SHACKLED, pinned high enough over my head to make my shoulders scream. There is no key. The qoru's touch makes the metal rust clean through when it's time to release the hold—until then, there is no escape. The metallic taste of blood fills my mouth.

A dream. This is a dream and I want to wake up. Need to wake up.

The overseer kicks my legs apart, the smell of blazing metal strong enough to overpower the stench of decay. I know that's impossible, but fear toys with my senses. Lashes are better than burns. Anything is better than burns. But I know there is no hope. These won't be the qoru's usual games, not today.

Wake up, wake up, wake up. I dig a fingernail into my palm. Wake up. Please.

The overseer snatches up a white-hot rod. Today is punishment.

I gasp awake, my body shaking, the bedding around me soaked with sweat. In the aftershocks of the nightmare, dream wraiths of mottled gray skin and round, lipless mouths drink their final fills of my terror. My heart pounds, my breath stretching my lungs.

A wet lupine tongue laps the inside of my ear, soft, worried yips brushing my soul. Outside, the Citadel bell tolls two hours past midnight. The middle of the night. As if I would dare return to sleep now.

I push myself up, hissing as my bruised muscles are forced into motion. Not the pleasant type of soreness that follows a heavy workout, but the deep hurt that seizes each motion, despite the salve Shade gently spread over my skin before shifting back into his wolf. All courtesy of the same source as the nightmare.

The wolf whines softly, prodding me with his snout.

"I'm all right," I mutter, trying and failing to shove two hundred pounds of animal away from me. If I'm not careful, Shade will damn the consequences and shift back into fae form just to heal my hurts. To care for me, like all the males do in their own way.

Like Coal did in the paddock this morning.

"I left him," I whisper, my heart squeezing.

The wolf blinks at me in sleepy confusion and tries to lick my ear again.

I swallow, wriggling off the bed, my blue nightshirt brushing my thighs. I left Coal shaking on his knees while echoes of his power still raced through my veins. I was unhappy about his tactics, his choices, and so I *left*. Stars.

No more. Enough of them doing what's best for me. It's time I did what's best for *them*. Starting with Coal.

Ignoring Shade's indignant whine and the cold air raising tiny bumps across my skin, I stalk into the corridor. The way today has gone thus far, I'll come out ahead even if Coal decides to tear me fiber from fiber. And if he does . . . I'd rather bear the brunt of Coal's fury than ever see the male on his knees again.

My breath stills as I knock on Coal's door, sweat coating my palms despite the chill. Around me, the sleeping suite mutters its usual nightly sounds of steady breathing and the dull whine of floorboards, the latter coming from our singularly nocturnal upstairs neighbors. Amidst it all, the soft rap of my knuckles against Coal's door sounds loud as thunder.

No answer.

I frown, my resolve faltering for a moment before I reclaim it and knock again. Louder.

Nothing. Not even when I put my ear against the door. Not Coal's breathing, not the creaking of a mattress, not even the echo of the tolling bell that seems to vibrate through every other wall. Truly *nothing* is coming from that door. As if something is purposely ensuring silence . . . just in case Coal wakes with a scream.

My pulse quickens. "Coal?" A final, futile attempt to get an answer.

I take a breath and let myself in.

8

LERA

*T*urning the knob, I step inside a large lantern-lit room. An *empty* lantern-lit room. The four-poster bed, a darker twin to my own, stands vacant and as disheveled as if someone had wrestled atop the covers. Thick curtains are open to the forest and a starlit sky. The scents of leather and steel hang thick enough to hint that Coal has been sharpening knives and oiling armor right in his own bedchamber.

And yet the room doesn't *feel* empty. On the contrary, the very air hums with energy, as if it too is curling its fingers into a fist.

"Co—" My words die as a large hand grips my neck. Air catches in my lungs then escapes in a strangled croak as my back slams into the wall. The door claps closed, the room shuddering with the impact. I blink, gasping as the confusion and fear seizing me morph into blinding fury.

Coal. Bare-chested and towering over me. His muscled arms pin me against the wall like a ragdoll. The perfect lines of his face, too beautiful to be anything but immortal, are tense as he glares down at me. His blond hair is down, brushing against his shoulders.

"Get the hell off me." I shove Coal's chest. The thin sheen of sweat coating his skin slicks my palms. My heart thunders, my breath coming in short, hard bursts. I'm going to kill the bastard, and then I'm going to rip off his balls and feed them to the crows. "You knew damn well it was me coming in."

Coal releases me, his chest heaving as he plants his hands on the wall just above my ears. Even now, in the middle of the night, strength and violence roll off Coal in waves. The heat of his body, clad only in loose cotton trousers that hang on the wings of his hips, soaks through my thin silk shift and spiders across my skin. Dipping his head down until his face is only inches from mine, Coal finally speaks. "I'm subtly suggesting that barging into my bedchamber uninvited is unwise."

Holding myself steady is a struggle. "Noted."

Coal's lips curl, showing his elongated canines, the sheer maleness of him making my thighs clench involuntarily. His eyes, blue ice even in the dim light, radiate power as loudly as his wide stance and spread shoulders. "What do you want, mortal?"

A fight, apparently. "I couldn't sleep."

"And why, pray tell, should that translate into you not letting *me* sleep?"

"Quit the horseshit, Coal. You weren't sleeping." Ducking beneath his arm, I wheel on the male, my hands on my hips. "I'm too damn sore and exhausted and sleep deprived to keep pretending that nothing happened this morning. So we are going to talk. *Now.*"

"Was I too hard on you, little Leralynn?" Coal purrs. "Are your bruises too deep?" His voice changes, becomes harsh. Cruel. "You walked yourself into that problem when you accepted the Elder Council's terms and became a Citadel initiate. Go whine to Shade or Tye, and leave me alone."

I wait for Coal's words to find their mark, but the memory of him kneeling on the sand is so potent that I hear his tossed words for the shield they are, see the breathtakingly brave male bleeding behind them. Straightening my spine, I stride deeper into Coal's room. Swords and knives with wicked-looking blades line the warrior's dresser, pieces of leather armor laid out beside them. Vambraces. A half-mended chest guard. A sword belt still shining with cleaning oil.

"You've been busy." I pick up one of the knives, its blade sharpened to a deadly edge. Resolve pulses through me, holding me up as I summon words I wish I could spare Coal from. "But then again, this is easier, isn't it? Focus on work. Blame *me*. Call *me* out for self-pitying words." Returning the weapon to its resting spot, I slowly turn toward Coal and find his eyes, the ghost of vulnerability in them tearing through my soul. I've always imagined that being on the receiving end of blows is hardest of all. Apparently not. I step toward Coal, mercilessly invading his space. "It is so much easier to shove me away than to face your own bloody darkness. To admit that *your* damn nightmares shred you to bits. And have been doing as much for three hundred years."

"Stop flattering yourself." Coal's voice is low, dangerous. "The only thing I feel just now is annoyed."

I snatch hold of Coal's wrist, the sores on it healing slowly after centuries of damage. I take a quick fortifying breath and torque the skin viciously. "Good thing this little bothers you," I say, holding his eyes through the pain and fury flashing in his gaze. "I'd hate for you to start whining."

Beneath my grip, Coal's pulse pounds against my skin. His lack of retort is as loud as a clap of thunder.

Too far. I've sliced too far, too quickly. Brought us too close to an abyss. My heart pounds, ice and fire crackling down my spine. I can feel Coal's bottled terror stretching the bounds of his control, and I know that one wrong breath will topple us both into a deadly chasm.

So I might as well jump. "Tell me, Coal," I say quietly, aiming my blow to shatter what's left of his shell and bare the male beneath. "What did the qoru do once they had your arms trapped and grew tired of whips and brands? I think I'd enjoy learning how one puts a fae warrior through his . . . paces."

Coal's eyes darken, his breath coming faster. "What do you want from me, Lera?"

"You." I swallow. "I want the true you, not the cleaned-up, gelded version that you pass off as truth to the world."

Something infinitesimal shifts in his face, all the warning I have before Coal jerks free of my hold. Gripping my hips with steel hands, he launches me backward.

My breath catches as my feet leave the ground, my body flying through the air. A moment later, the backs of my thighs strike Coal's bed, my upper body falling atop the mattress. I struggle to push myself upright, but Coal pounces before I can move.

My heart gallops, my mouth drying as Coal's powerful legs wrap around mine like grapevines. Forearms braced against the mattress, the warrior looms over me, the thick muscles along his arms coiled with tension, the air between us hot from fury and sweat. "You don't want the true me," he growls, his canines flashing in the starlight. "You'd little like it. If you even survived it."

Panic bubbles inside me even as . . . as a jolt of absurd

need flashes through my core. I draw a shuddering breath, anchoring myself to reality.

"I suggest you stop prying, mortal." Coal's voice is a soft rumble, his body, his essence, filling the entire chamber. Taking all of the room's air for itself. As if the male I thought I knew was but a mask concealing a power too grand to contend with. "You know nothing of what lurks in my thoughts. Of what my instincts will do to you if I let them loose." Coal pauses, arching his hips such that the grapevine hold his legs have on mine extends me painfully. His hardness presses down into my mound. "Believe me when I say it will be nothing like your games with Shade."

I shudder, my terror slamming against an equal force of sudden, erratic desire, the resulting explosion leaving me dazed. Wrong. Everything about this is wrong. Especially the flames consuming my body, the wetness all but streaming down my thighs.

This isn't what I came here for. Isn't something I should like. Isn't *right*.

"I will count to three." Coal swallows, his arms now trembling with the effort of holding rock-still above me. "And by the time I'm done, you are going to be out of this room. If you are not . . . then I imagine you will be a great deal more sore in the morning. Because I am a breath away from showing you exactly what happens when my control falters. And we both know that is not what you want."

Stars. What *do* I want? I can't think. Can barely breathe. I should get out of this room, run as fast as I can. Never look back. My body pulses, the throbbing in my chest sliding lower with each dizzying breath. My thighs quiver. My body defying my mind, as I defy Coal's words.

"One," Coal says.

I draw a breath, my gaze skittering across him. Large and powerful and dark. Raw.

"In case you've not worked it out, my room is warded to contain sound. No one will hear your screams." Coal's words are cold and hard.

My sex aches. My mind searches for escape. I brace my hands on the bed—the path to the door is wide open to me. Not for long, but for now.

Coal follows my gaze, nodding approvingly. *Yes*, his flashing eyes tell me. *Yes, go. Leave. RUN.* "Two."

9

COAL

"Two," Coal said, his body trembling. Keeping himself up on his forearms, he glared at the mortal trapped beneath him. The part of him that could still think begged her to run. The rest of him stared in breath-halting disbelief at the female he'd wanted since they first shared a saddle, now lying splayed open upon his bed.

Lera was on her back, the thin blue silk of her nightgown clinging to her round breasts, smooth abdomen, and tight, perfectly curved hips. Worse still, with Coal's legs pinning hers in a grapevine vice, the fabric of Lera's shift had ridden up her thighs. Up her hips. Wisps of the female's hair—coiled tufts the same fiery brown color as their counterparts on her head —peeked from beneath the dislodged hem. Between the lantern, the stars, and his own immortal sight, Coal could see beads of moisture hanging on those tufts, like droplets on the side of a sweating glass of wine.

Stars.

Coal shuddered, the scent of Lera's arousal waking his

senses. A fanciful, misguided arousal that somehow failed to understand the monster only inches away from it. Coal's pulse thumped against his ribs, an echo to the one stretching his balls.

Lera squirmed beneath him. Too small, too mortal, too damn breakable for what Coal's cock screamed to do.

He needed for Lera to leave. No, not just leave. *Run.* To never, ever return to his bedchamber, especially not alone and clad in little more than feisty darkness. Coal smelled it on her, the spice of fight and grit that spiked her lilac scent and made his head swim with need. Made his cock harden so fiercely that pain shot from it through his thighs.

Lera's liquid brown gaze darted toward the door as she finally, *finally* understood the need for escape. It'd certainly taken her long enough. Stars, one would think that after what he'd done to the female that morning, she'd be giving him a wide berth for a year.

Plainly, Lera was no normal being.

Coal nodded, the final count harsh on his lips. "Three."

Lera shoved Coal away. His body screamed its protest as he yielded, his muscles hating to release their prey but—thank the stars—obeying. For a moment, all Coal could do was kneel on the bed and focus on his breath, on keeping himself from grabbing Lera's hair and dragging her right back to him. He wanted to yell that she move faster, that his restraint was thinning to nothing, but even that would take too much concentration.

Breathe. He needed to breathe. He—

Lera pounced on him. Shoved Coal onto his back and straddled his chest with her wickedly moist thighs. She pinned his shoulders with her hands, her nails digging into his naked flesh, sending a bolt of pain and desire through him. Igniting his magic like a match thrown into a pile of dry hay.

Coal's body quivered with panting breaths, his hands digging into the covers as Lera loomed over him, her auburn hair brushing his shoulders. Her eyes aflame.

"Is this the part where I was supposed to run?" she whispered into his ear. "Just so I know."

Coal's need exploded. Stars speckling his vision, he grabbed Lera's hips and threw her off him so hard that the female was airborne for the instant it took him to recapture her body. To propel her off the bed and toward the wall.

Coal twisted to take the crash of impact himself as their bodies hit the hard stone, then twisted again to pin Lera's back to the wall. The *throb, throb, throb* of his cock driving all thoughts into a dark abyss, Coal clamped his hand over Lera's wrists and forced them up high above her head.

Lera opened her mouth. To moan or to scream, Coal didn't know. Didn't care. He'd wanted her from the moment her soft backside first pressed against his cock on Czar's back, but he'd *needed* her from the moment she first sparred with him, taking his blows with defiance, meeting his darkness with brilliant fire. And by the stars, he'd have her now.

Capturing Lera's open lips, Coal drove his mouth over hers, swallowing her gasp. His tongue pierced the opening between her teeth and stroked her mouth as hard as his cock throbbed. As hard as the burn of waking magic that scorched his nerves.

All the times Coal had dreamt of tasting the mortal—and there had been many—he'd imagined her to taste sweet, innocent. But he'd been wrong. Lera tasted of power. Power and violence and steel. Lera tasted of Coal's own magic.

Impossible. Illogical. Undeniable.

Coal's breath caught then painfully filled his lungs.

The female pulled against his grip, struggling to free herself from his living restraints. Not a mortal's feeble jerk, but one filled with the same preternatural strength that they'd shared in the second trial. No. Not the same. Stronger. So, so much stronger. Power hummed under Lera's skin, radiating from each of her muscles. And that was after just one kiss. Coal's heart stuttered.

Which was all the leeway the girl needed.

Twisting her wrists against Coal's thumbs, Lera broke free of his hold. Her mouth still locked with his, she jerked them around, slamming Coal's back into the wall in her place. Driving into him hard enough that his bones rattled from the impact. Releasing Coal's mouth, Lera glared up at him, her eyes . . . usually a stunning brown, but now filled with speckles of silver magic, sparkling like tiny stars over the irises.

Not a weak, fragile human, but an equal. A predator to be conquered.

Lera's nails raked across Coal's chest possessively, ripping skin. Marking him.

A roar formed inside his soul and spread through his body, the untamed beast inside him yanking against its tether. Coal knew that beast, made of power and magic. When the qoru had chained him, bled him, pinned him against the wall and used him for sport, the magic inside Coal had roared this way too, right before turning him into a beast capable of meeting his owners blow for blow.

The beast had let Coal survive Mors. And now it set its predatory sights on the female, drowning out the last of Coal's better sense.

Coal yanked on Lera's right wrist, bending it until her

knees buckled. Pulling the wrist across her body, he twisted the female around and shoved her chest into the wall.

With Lera's arm now pinned into the small of her back, Coal pressed himself against her, his hard, sensitive cock striking her backside. Coal's nostrils flared, Lera's scent, her arousal, heating his blood. Bringing up his knee, he forced it between her legs, wedging her thighs apart until she was splayed open before him.

Lera's heart pounded—Coal could feel it through the press of their flesh. Dropping his free hand down, he gave no warning before plunging two fingers deep into her sex.

Wet, flaming slickness met him, Lera's body begging for him even as she struggled to get free. A perfect, powerful body whose every contraction made stars dance before Coal's eyes.

Coal slipped his hand out of her long enough to free himself, his cock hard and dripping. Screaming with need. With no breath left, he thrust forward, sheathing himself in Lera's wicked tightness.

10

LERA

I gasp as Coal thrusts into me, the great length of him filling my body as his equally great power fills my essence. Magic explodes inside me, my sex tightening around Coal. My shoulder burns where he has my arm twisted behind me, but even the pain is a rumble that wakes my senses, somehow making the roaring pleasure in my sex even more vivid.

The power of Coal's thrusts brings me to my toes, his hot breath scorching the back of my neck. My heart pounds, the energy exploding between us ready to rip the room into shreds.

I feel . . . strong. Stronger than I did in the ring this morning. Stronger than I've ever felt in my life. As if a fog has lifted from the bridge linking Coal and me, revealing Coal's power in all its intoxicating, undiluted glory.

Shoving away from the wall, I knock us both backward, caring nothing for what might be in the way. We crash onto the hard floor, my body screaming its fury over the sudden, unintended loss of Coal's cock. I scramble to pull him back into me, my flailing limbs connecting with something that sends a rain of weapons and armor clattering down to the stone floor.

Coal grips my hair as he climbs to his knees. His blue eyes flash with specks of black and purple, and as our gazes meet, images of gray-skinned qoru flash in the aching depths of my mind.

Our *other* connection surfacing to play, the fog fighting to reclaim its throne.

Panic flashes in Coal's gaze, the images coming faster now. Shackles. Pain. The dampened sounds of those bent-the-wrong-way legs approaching in the Gloom. Fear and fight.

This close, I feel Coal's desperate, bloodcurdling struggle to stay in the present. A fight that the black specks in his eyes say he is losing. My heart breaks.

"Leave," Coal pants, his jaw clenched, his muscles quivering, his hair gleaming silver in the moonlight. "Break for the door and run."

Run before I see more, before what remains of Coal's control fails. This is what the male's every moment is like, I realize with sudden shock. A struggle to keep his past shoved down to a dark corner of his mind. To protect the world—and me—from himself.

"There are two of us to fight the qoru now," I shout into Coal's face. "Try to hoard them all for yourself and I will tear open your throat." I mean it too, drunk as I am on our shared power. Shared darkness. I want Coal. With all his jagged edges, his raw, brutal strength that makes me unable to stay still for my throbbing need.

Purple flashes in Coal's eyes. With a growl, he yanks me up and throws me away from him. A dull pain I don't truly feel tells me I've struck something—likely the dresser, given its subsequent crash, drawers slipping free.

I recover into a crouch. Bending my knees, I lower my head and step around Coal, aiming my shoulder for the bend of his hips. Coal's flesh, fully naked, glistens with sweat. Muscles I've never seen before flicker and bulge under his tawny skin as he crouches across from me. For an instant, my gaze catches on the taut, wet length of him, noting that it belongs inside me. By the time the thought penetrates, I'm already moving.

My shoulder strikes Coal with more speed and force than I thought possible, the impact echoing gloriously through me.

Coal absorbs the blow, his lithe body spinning with the force of my strike, turning the momentum to his own purposes. His heavy hand shoves between my shoulder blades, propelling me toward his bed.

I slam into the foot of the bed, gasping as the male bends me over it. With a rough pull, Coal rips the silk nightshift off my back, cold air brushing my exposed shoulder blades and my raised, bared backside.

One hand sliding to the nape of my neck, Coal rakes the other possessively over my skin, reaching down to grip my breast with his calloused palm.

I whimper.

"Quiet," Coal commands, as if I can control the sounds his body is calling forth from mine. The hand on my breast squeezes punishingly, and I gasp from the sudden pain that zings from my nipple straight to my apex, waking me with brutal efficiency.

Grabbing my shoulder, Coal flips me over to face him. Shackling both my wrists with one hand, he looms over me, his free palm engulfing my breast again, his hard cock pressing against my mound.

Gray skin flashes in my mind, sending a streak of terror through my core.

Coal grips my face at once, forcing my eyes to meet his. The male's blue-purple gaze opens my soul. Bares his to me in return. Coal saw the qoru too. But now—now we see each other.

My eyes widen with understanding. Whether stretching through the nightmares' fog or passion's light, it is this raw, vulnerable intensity that forges the link between us. That, for good or ill, makes Coal's magic sing loudly enough for me to echo.

Coal's mouth descends upon mine, hard and desperate, his masculine musk flooding my senses. He's sharing his strength with me, his magic, giving me all of himself to arm me against darkness. Accepting my strength in return. And I love him for it.

When our air is gone and my lungs scream for breath, Coal pulls away from the kiss.

At once, my mouth misses the invasion of his, empty without his warmth filling it. I flex my head up and sink my teeth into Coal's neck. "Get back where you belong," I rasp, the emptiness inside me roaring.

A snort, then Coal flips me right back over the foot of the bed. Parting my thighs with his knees, the male buries himself inside me with a hard, well-aimed stroke. I moan as my body stretches to accommodate his length, but Coal gives no quarter. Hands braced on the crests of my hips, he starts pumping, hitting my insides so deep that I feel his reverberations through my core. My moans and pants fill the room, each one fueling Coal's cock, making his strokes wilder, harder.

My sex tenses around him, each *slap, slap, slap* of Coal's pelvis against my backside bringing me one step closer to the edge. The sheer size of him, the powerful thrusts, the rub of his throbbing cock along my channel's ridges . . . Stars. Waves of desire pound my body, a storm of growing, unbearable need. My fingers grip the sheets, my voice filling the air. "More."

One of Coal's hands rips free of my hip and tangles itself in my hair. He yanks my head up, the pain in my scalp as excruciating as the need of my swollen sex, my body instinctively slamming back into his just as—

All of my muscles seem to tense at once, my body arching from the pressure. The magic pulsing through my veins rattles every frayed nerve. Around my apex, a swirling, excruciating tornado twists tighter and deeper. Harder. Clenching around Coal's fullness, my sex finally explodes into rippling, painful pleasure, and I scream.

My breathing—once I find it again—comes in sharp, quick pants.

Behind me, Coal groans with his own release, his warmth filling my body. And for one glorious second, he holds me there against his hard chest, my head resting on his shoulder, our warmth and sweat mingling.

Then he lowers me back to the bed and withdraws in a cold instant, chilly air swirling against my back.

I draw a shuddering breath and crawl onto the bed, my body still trembling from drunken fatigue. By the time I've collected myself, Coal is in the middle of the chamber, his feet set apart on the floor as he stares at me with wide eyes, glistening chest heaving.

I blink at his smooth body then survey the room. The dresser is toppled, the weapons and leather strewn across the ground. My nightshirt is destroyed, little more than a rag. Swallowing, I pull Coal's sheet over me.

His dazed blue eyes rake over me, searching for something. "I'll . . . I'll get Tye," he says gruffly.

11

LERA

"*W*hat?" The slightly drunk fatigue clears in a heartbeat. "Why the hell would you get Tye?"

Coal crosses his arms but makes no move toward the bed where we just joined. "Because he knows what to do now."

"What is there to do now?" I ask.

"I. Don't. Know." Coal enunciates each word as if speaking to someone hard of hearing. "I've . . . I've only paid for my pleasure before. This isn't something I've done for . . . I don't know if you are all right."

"Have you considered asking me?"

"No." His jaw works. "Are you all right?"

"No."

Coal throws up his arms. "Then why the bloody hell are we having this conversation?" He spins on his heels, grabs his pants off the floor, and strides out of the room before I can stop him.

My face flames. A moment ago, all I wanted was to feel

73

Coal beside me. Now I just want to sink into the ground or throttle the bastard. Or both.

I pull the covers higher over my neck, scanning the room to see if I can manage to disappear before the males return. I pull up my knees, resting my forehead against them for a long heartbeat before throwing off the sheets altogether.

I'm not some damsel in need of bloody assistance. I was the one who came here. Who wanted him. Who took my pleasure, just as much as Coal did. Took more than he was ready to give, if I'm honest. The connection, the magic . . . It was more than I was prepared for. More than I ever felt when we shared his memories. I rub my hand over my face. Rising from the bed, I stride over to what's left of Coal's dresser, pull out one of the half-fallen drawers, and empty its contents onto the floor. Before I can locate a shift amid the mess, the door behind me opens and two males, both wearing loose breeches, step inside.

"Why are you standing there naked?" Coal asks.

"I imagine because somewhere between her coming into the room and you leaving, you did something requiring her clothes to be removed," Tye says, rubbing sleep from his eyes. His red hair stands up in messy spikes that would be adorable under any other circumstances.

"What's left of my nightshirt is somewhere on the floor," I say primly, making no move to cover myself as Coal's nostrils flare. After taking a moment of perverse enjoyment in the male's discomfort, I pull one of his shirts from the wreckage and slip it over my head. Coal's metallic musk fills my nose as the cloth settles over me, the hem so long that it brushes my knees.

"Why am I here?" Tye asks, looking between me and Coal. "It seems you two have everything under control."

"There is nothing bloody under control," Coal growls.

"That's good too." Tye turns to Coal, opening his arms. "What, pray tell, do you want me to do?"

"Hug her," Coal demands, gesturing toward me brusquely.

"What?" Tye and I say together.

"That's what you do with females after coupling with them. I don't. So I'm delegating."

"One, you can't delegate hugging, Coal," I tell him. "And two, what makes you think I even want that from you?"

"I hurt you." His jaw is tight, his fist seeming ready to strike a wall.

"Yes." I straighten my shirt. "It was good for me too. Thank you for asking."

"Bloody stars, I don't believe we are having this conversation," Tye groans. "Can I assume that all involved enjoyed themselves until there wasn't anything left to enjoy?" He waits the briefest of moments before nodding to no one in particular. "Then figure out the bloody aftermath without me. So long as I can have the lass tomorrow to show her everything you did wrong."

Coal grabs Tye's wrist. "What are we supposed to do now?" he asks. Demands.

Tye leans close to the warrior, his face only inches away as he snarls right back at him. "Practice." Pulling back, Tye leaves, slamming the door in his wake.

I blink once at the slammed door then start toward it, Coal's large shirt tickling my thighs. Stars. The size of the male . . . everywhere. The fabric smells of soap and cleanliness, while the room I'm leaving is anything but. Overturned dresser, cracked bedpost, weapons scattered on the floor. I trip on a sword belt and swallow a curse.

"Where are you going?" Coal asks behind me, his voice gravelly.

Away from here. Back to my room. Outside. I don't know. With my heart returning to its normal rate, the strength is draining from my body, leaving behind the aftermath of what we did.

"Nowhere in particular," I say over my shoulder, my voice wavering. What happened between us, it was little but sport to him. A game. And it *was* fun, the exhilaration of it. The . . . the ending was certainly worth the ramp-up. My body heats in memory of what just happened, my bones melting with desire for a single moment—before the aftermath crashes into me again like an avalanche. If was fun, and now, like a good sparring session, it's over. Coal made that clear enough. I should be glad he isn't heading for the baths. I swat a loose strand of hair from my face. "I'm just leaving here."

"Don't." Coal's voice is hard, as if he can't decide whether he's asking a favor or issuing an order.

I turn slowly, facing the male standing half-naked in the lantern light. Coal looks like he's just come out of battle, his blond hair wild, sweat coating his skin, and a deep, still-bleeding gash crossing from his shoulder over the hard swell of his pectoral and stopping dangerously close to his nipple.

Coal's gaze follows mine. He stares at the blood for a moment, a small smile tugging at the corner of his mouth. His lower part twitches in confirmation of having enjoyed the experience leading up to that particular injury.

Heat floods my cheeks as an answering pang pulses between my legs. What we did . . . what he did to me. What I did to him. The magic and power that roared through us both. So right. And so very wrong. It was wrong to have enjoyed it. I turn back to the door and stride toward it.

The room swims, the magic draining from me like water through a sieve. I only realize Coal has moved when the floor shifts and the male's solid arms catch me before the chamber dumps me onto its floor.

With one arm behind my shoulder blades and the other supporting my knees, Coal returns me to his bed, settling me with surprising gentleness on the mussed sheets. After a heartbeat of hesitation, he retrieves the fallen blanket and covers me with it. "Sleep here tonight, mortal."

I open my mouth to protest but the words shift to a different sort when, instead of settling down on the mattress beside me, Coal lies down on the floor. "What are you doing?"

"I told you to remain in my chamber," Coal says matter-of-factly. "It seems proper to give you the bed."

"It seems proper for you to get your ass into said bed first," I say, my indignation waking me for a moment.

Coal stiffens.

I sigh, my jaw clenching hard enough that it's an effort of will to get it to move. "You need not hug me, Coal," I say, turning my back to him in emphasis. Trying to sound as if Coal's revulsion at the thought of brushing up against me is of no consequence. "You don't have to touch me at all. But for the sake of my ethics, I'd appreciate it if you didn't stretch out on a stone floor either."

After a moment I feel the bed shift, Coal's body settling reluctantly on the other side of the mattress. As I drift off into sleep, I realize that the heavy weight of the male's arm has somehow settled across me, while Coal himself slumbers with deep, easy breaths.

～

I WAKE to shooting pain scorching my shoulder and streaking along my body. My shoulder, my back, my ribs. As if I've been in battle. Which, given the state of the dresser, is rather close to reality.

Beside me, Coal is sleeping on his stomach, one heavy arm draped over my hips as his back rises and falls in a deep, slow rhythm, his sculpted muscles shifting slightly with each inhalation. I've never seen the warrior sleep calmly before, I realize. Even when traveling, Coal woke at the slightest movement, the merest of sounds. Now, his beautiful face, framed by a wild mane of blond hair, looks content. Amidst Coal's scars, I find fresh gashes and bruises that make my face heat with memory. Four parallel lines slashing across Coal's scapula like claw marks are half-healed already.

Unlike me.

I shut my eyes, trying to strategize a means of moving that will not make me scream. With last night's intense connection to Coal broken, the last of his magic has drained from my veins overnight, the preternatural strength and resilience I echoed now completely gone. I go to slide out from under the male's arm and hiss as the motion jostles my shoulder.

Coal wakes in an instant, his blue eyes clear and surveying the world for danger before finding it beneath his own hand. He pulls back from me quickly, as if drawing back from a hornet's nest.

Right. Fine. No matter. At least with him awake, I need not be subtle about moving. Wishing the door were much closer to the bed, I try to gather my legs beneath me.

Coal's heavy palms still my torso before I can move. His nostrils flare delicately as he takes in my scent. Then he curses colorfully. "How bad is it, mortal?" he demands.

"Good morning to you too," I mutter.

Coal pulls the blanket off me, ignoring my indignant squeak as he rips his shirt off my body as well. His calloused and impossibly gentle hands probe along my skin. "I think I cracked several ribs," he whispers, the color gone from his face. "As for your shoulder . . ." He flexes the joint, drawing another gasp from my throat. "Stars, mortal. It's a hair away from dislocation."

Broken ribs? Dislocated shoulder? I blink. "How—"

"How? Do you truly require a recap?" Coal runs his hands through his loose hair then turns tightly to sink his fist into the already cracked bedpost. His body trembles, his hands clenched as his gaze brushes my body again. "I don't know what to say," he says softly. "You can exact whatever retribution you wish, but we both know it won't be enough. I've hurt—I've *injured* you, mortal. There isn't a way to make it right."

"What the hell are you talking about?" I wince, shifting myself into a sitting position. "First, there were two of us playing yesterday. And second, how come you aren't ever this upset about walloping me in training?"

Coal blinks at the question, his crystal-blue eyes opening and closing like an owl's. "Because when we train, I hit what I'm aiming for." He lowers his head, his shoulders dropping. "That was not the case last night. I wasn't in control."

No. Neither of us was. "I thought that was the whole point," I mutter. I reach toward Coal but my hand finds empty air as the male vaults off the bed and strides to the door, from which I now hear low lupine whines intercepted with displeased growls.

"That's Shade," Coal says, confirming my suspicions. "He

cannot hear us, but his wolf smells his mate hurt. And that I hurt her."

Before I can point out that this seems like a very good reason to keep the door shut, Coal pulls it open.

Two hundred pounds of angry predator rushes through the opening and crosses the room in two large leaps, knocking Coal flat on his back. The door slamming closed in his wake, Shade lands on the bed beside me, regaining his fae form in a flash of furious light. His nostrils flare, his yellow gaze fevered as he brushes my cheek. His masculine face turns deadly as he spins on Coal, eyes flashing with bloodthirst.

A shiver runs down my spine. My heart pounds as the air between the males crackles. I try and fail to rise, my chest clenching around lungs that suddenly have trouble drawing air. "Stop it, you idiots!"

Still on the floor, Coal's tortured gaze lifts to Shade's, who advances with predatory slowness.

Coal picks himself up from the stone. For a horrifying heartbeat, the certainty that the two will truly try to kill each other echoes like thunder through my bones. Then lightning strikes with a reality that's more chilling still.

Instead of getting to his feet, Coal rises only as far as his knees. Shoulders spread, head down, hands locked in the small of his back.

Shade draws back a fist, taking aim at Coal's jaw. My breath catches. Shade's knuckles crack against Coal's face, the kneeling male grunting from the blow but never taking his hands from behind him, not even as blood runs from his split lip onto the floor.

"Don't you dare hit him again!" I call, though neither male gives any sign of having heard me.

Showing his teeth, Shade kicks Coal's unprotected abdomen, doubling the male over.

When Shade pulls back for the next blow, I grit my teeth, wrap the sheet around me, and sprint to the door. My body screams, my muscles giving out just as I crack it open enough to break Coal's soundproofing wards and bellow for River with all the breath I have left.

LERA

"What's happened?" River demands, crouching with Autumn beside me in the hallway while Tye sprints past us into the room, catches Shade's wrist mid-blow, and throws the male into the closest wall. I cringe at the sound of a body hitting stone and then again as the last of Coal's drawers topples from the overturned dresser. River's gray eyes narrow and his nostrils flare, the scents of injury and sex no doubt filling his nose like perfume. "We've a trial we can't fail in less than a week's time, and one of my quint members can barely stand up. I want to know what *exactly* happened."

"I'm hardly what Autumn would call intelligent," Tye calls, standing his ground between the still-kneeling Coal and furiously panting Shade, "but it seems that Coal not only bedded Shade's mate but had a really good time doing it."

Coal growls. "I did not have a good time."

"What?" I rise onto my elbow, my face hot.

Tye cuts his eyes down toward the male. "Please keep

talking Coal. You're making the rest of us look great in comparison."

Shade rises, his bare chest heaving as he shows his teeth to both Tye and Coal then stalks to me. River holds his ground, but Shade's golden eyes focus on mine to the exclusion of the world. He crouches beside me, black hair falling around his worried face, and my breath stills, my heart pounding against hurt ribs.

Shade's earthy scent caresses me as his fingers touch my face, too gentle for the large warrior. A tingle touches my skin and I jerk back from the wolf shifter's hand, a hiss escaping my lips.

Shade flinches. "I won't hurt you, cub," he whispers. "Not you. Not ever."

"I know." I swallow, longing to rest my aching head in the hollow of his shoulder, right between the bulging muscles of his arm and hard squares of his chest. I want to be in Shade's arms. Want to be in all of their arms. But this isn't the time. Putting on what I hope is a stern voice, despite the indignity of cowering on the floor dressed in nothing but a bedsheet, I gently push his hand away. "You are going to hurt yourself. I felt you reach for your magic."

Shade's jaw tightens and he reaches forward again, the strain of calling upon his power enough to make beads of sweat rise on his brow. "I will make my own decisions about my magic."

I grab his wrist. "Like hell you will."

"Welcome to my world," River mutters darkly behind me.

I release Shade's wrist, blinking at the commander. He looks as terrible as I feel, the weight he carries on his broad shoulders echoing in his eyes as he takes in the space around him. Shade, dark with fury over being denied killing himself.

Coal, kneeling and bloody. Me, unable to sit up. Tye, standing in the middle of it all, struggling to grin over the concern clouding his face. Autumn, looking on with a tension that tells me Kora's quint has yet to return.

River's world. The one that he's been desperately trying to keep from collapsing around our ears. Except . . . I raise my chin, meeting River's eyes. "Not yours, River," I say quietly. "*Ours*. I'm just as responsible for the quint as you are."

"That's—"

Autumn puts a hand on her brother's arm to stop him. "Lera is a weaver," she says softly. "There are some things only she can do."

River says nothing, running his hands along my body in the way Coal did earlier. Checking for injuries and coming up with a list that turns his gray eyes dark. "Can you make it to the infirmary?" he asks with a detachment that promises a less pleasant conversation to come. "Or do we need to fetch a healer here?"

Shade growls. "No one is healing Lera but me."

"Oh, be quiet, all of you," Autumn huffs, striding past us into Coal's room. Bracing her hands on the hips of her coral silk pants, she studies both the wreckage and the wrecked with an academic's curious gaze. In the bright light of morning, I see it suddenly through her sharp eyes—a literal war zone. "When did this happen?" she asks finally, waving a slender hand between Coal and me.

"Last night," Coal says. "Around two."

"Two." Hands back on her hips, Autumn turns to meet each of the males' gazes in turn. "And which amongst you imagine that Coal actually injured a helpless female and then kept her locked up for five hours in his bedchamber?"

My spine straightens, the motion making me wince. "I'm not a helpless female."

"My point exactly," Autumn says primly. "But it will take these oafs a few more minutes to work that out. If you rush them, they'll sprain their brains. An organ that some of them"—she looks pointedly at Coal and Shade—"have not used in some time."

Coal shuts his eyes, his pale skin turning a shade of red that would be amusing if he weren't also bleeding. "Our coupling opened my magic for Lera's echo." He rubs his face. "She was strong. Stronger than . . . She did not appear injured at the time we—"

"Jumped all over each other like a pair of bizzerked rabbits?" Tye supplies helpfully.

I grab the closest thing to me—which happens to be Coal's boot, right across the room's threshold—and chuck it at Tye's chest. An exercise that makes me grunt in more pain than he does.

Coal turns away from Tye, his eyes fully on Autumn. "Lera appeared sore when we were done, but not injured—though perhaps my own senses were muddled by then. By morning, whatever magic she'd been echoing faded, and with it, the true extent of her injuries surfaced. Her body now shows the effects of our activity as a mortal's would."

Before the last words are out of Coal's mouth, Tye kneels beside me and presses his lips against mine, his delicious pine-and-citrus scent surrounding me. I'm startled enough to kiss him back before coming to my senses.

"What the hell are you doing?" River demands.

"If coupling with Coal made Lilac Girl a temporary fae, it seems prudent to check whether kissing me might do the same," Tye says over his shoulder, holding my face in both hands as he speaks.

"I don't think it works that way," I tell the male. "We have kissed before, you know."

"Stop interfering with the scientific method," Tye declares, his attention now fully on my face. Before I can protest, he clamps his mouth over mine, sliding his hands down to pin my arms against my sides. His tongue fills my mouth, decisive and deft as it explores. As it brushes everything, marking it as its own.

Behind me, River clears his throat, and Tye pulls away with a sigh, his emerald eyes flashing with feline self-content.

"Did it work?" River asks dryly. "Is Leralynn healed?"

"She certainly is," Tye says. "Can you imagine waking up with the memory of Coal's kiss and no one to improve upon it?"

"No," says River. "I neither can nor wish to." He turns to Autumn. "I presume you are about to say that Leralynn needs Coal's magic, specifically, to heal?"

The female nods, her silver-blond braids swinging. "Like the rest of you, when Coal and Lera connect, she is able to echo his power. Unlike the rest of you, Coal's magic is turned inward—making him stronger, faster, a quicker healer than other fae—and thus can affect Lera's body similarly. Make her stronger, help her heal faster. That said—" Autumn pauses, her gray eyes getting that glazed, excited look that I've learned heralds a new theory. "That said, while the link between Coal and Lera is unique, I would think that coupling with any of you should strengthen Lera's ability to control your individual magic stream. Strengthening your physical bond in turn strengthens your magical bond."

I feel my eyes widen.

Autumn grins, her voice quickening. "The connection between body and magic is well known—it's the reason you use physical gestures to help guide your magic and why you train for physical endurance to enhance your magical reserves. In that light, it makes simple sense that Lera could control Shade's healing magic more effectively than Tye's fire or River's earth affinity. She and Shade had already coupled by that point."

Silence.

Utter, face-burning silence.

"If the next words out of your mouth, Autumn, include 'schedule,' 'evaluation,' or 'comparable variable,'" River says finally, "I will smother you with a pillow in your sleep. Understand?"

Autumn's pointed ears turn a pretty shade of pink.

Rubbing my hands over my face, I push Autumn's words to arm's length, their implications too overwhelming to deal with just now. One problem at a time. For the moment, the active-problem slot is firmly reserved for a hurt shoulder and cracked ribs.

"Can all of you leave, please?" I say, using the wall to climb to my feet and ignoring the five immediate sounds of protest. Six, if I count my own body's reaction. "Correction, can all of you but Coal please leave?"

No one does.

Fine.

Squinting into the light coming through Coal's open window, I knot the sheet around me in a makeshift dress and start my way across the room. Shade steps toward me but I shake my head, the movement nearly splitting my skull. For a moment, the tanned male looks like he'll protest, but Tye puts a hand on his shoulder, keeping the shifter at bay.

Coal kneels still. His gaze is on the floor when I stop beside him, the blood from his split lip dripping onto the stone. He looks more wounded than he did after the whipping, every line of muscle in his body rigid. Stiff with self-reproach. A condemnation heavier than any words, any swing of Shade's fist.

The silence of the room grows heavier with each heartbeat.

Taking a fortifying breath, I lower to my knees, unable to hold back a whimper as the movement jostles cracked ribs. Behind me, I hear Shade's sharp intake of breath. Coal, on the other hand, remains still as stone.

"Coal."

Vulnerable blue eyes turn up to meet mine. "Whatever retribution you wish to—"

"I don't need retribution." Putting a hand on Coal's cheek, I capture the warrior's gaze. "I need *you*." I search for words that Coal will hear, respect. "I need your help to heal."

He blinks for a moment, digesting my words, glancing at Autumn for confirmation. His throat bobs. "If you believe my magic can help, then it is yours," he says softly. "But use my memories to bridge into it. It's more controlled—it's safer that way."

"Safer for me, maybe, but not for you. I don't need safer," I whisper back, aware of the many eyes watching our every move. "We did this. We'll fix it." Despite the kiss Tye just took, this moment still feels frighteningly raw. Naked. Raising my other hand, I cup the back of Coal's head and press my mouth over his.

Coal's eyes jerk up, and for an instant I taste nothing but surprise and blood. His arms, still clasped behind his back, twitch but stay locked. Beneath his bare, muscled chest, the warrior's heart beats so hard that I can feel it pumping as vividly as the heat coming off his flesh and the metallic scent that wraps around him like armor.

I press harder and Coal's mouth responds on instinct, his lips claiming mine with a harsh power that sparks a firefly of magic inside my chest.

The male pulls back with a gasp, his blue eyes wide, and I nod my confirmation. Yes. I felt it. Just as he did.

I reach for him again to continue, wincing as I bend too far and shooting pain pierces my ribs. The room tilts.

Coal's arms shoot out from behind his back at once, bracing my shoulder blades. Steadying me. Coal's steel support anchors me to him while he grips my eyes and slips one hand to the back of my head. His fingers wrap possessively in my hair, taking charge with the same singular purpose that he carries into a sparring ring. Giving me no time to breathe, Coal's mouth descends upon mine. A hard, visceral assault that is perfectly Coal. Perfectly us.

I respond in kind, my own tongue plunging into his bruised mouth. My scalp tingles where Coal's hand pulls my hair, his other hand both supporting my weight and preventing escape. My hands dig into his shoulders, my nails raking along his skin as I feel his magic echoing inside me.

Pulsing power, frighteningly strong and familiar, blossoms in my chest before spreading through my body, the energy more potent than any wine. A door thrown open. A dam lifted. My heart quickens as I feel yet another sensation.

Coal's essence challenging mine, daring me to yield. Our magic's brewing battle for dominance sings sweetly through my veins. Waking my nerves. Making me strong. Alive.

Tye whistles. Grunts in pain. Shuts up.

An audience. I'd forgotten about them. I shudder, my

magic tripping over itself, pulling back from its tangle with Coal's. Even in front of our own quint, the intimacy of the connection strips me naked. Exposed.

Coal's grip on me tightens, his tongue raking possessively through my mouth. Fighting for my focus. Fighting for me and the magic simmering in my veins.

My chest heaves as we finally pull away, my hands braced on my knees. Coal wipes the back of his hand over his lip, the gash in it smaller than it was before. My own body is battered still, but with vines of magic reinforcing the joints and bones, it no longer feels frail. Coal extends his hand and we rise together, our bodies helping each other come erect in a suddenly empty room.

13

LERA

*O*nce my ribs no longer threaten to puncture a lung each time I take a step—at least for the brief window of time that Coal's magic still simmers in my blood—Autumn walks me to the Citadel's infirmary, a low ivy-covered building near the library. The cheerful blue sky and nodding flowers mock my insides as we make painfully slow progress across the grounds, the clusters of fae we pass watching me unabashedly and whispering the moment we're past.

"Ignore the idiots," Autumn says quietly after the third such encounter, then louder, "They've never trained hard enough to injure themselves."

"If they knew what *training* did this, it might motivate a great deal of study." My cheeks heat when I realize I said the thought out loud. I clear my throat. But the small perk in Autumn's step says it's too late to backtrack.

"So," Autumn says, shooting me a sideways glance. "Coal."

"Coal," I echo flatly.

uncomfortable walking into the supper hall naked, though that little seems a problem at other times, aye?"

My cheeks flush and Tye chuckles softly, running a knuckle across my cheek in a way that sends a blaze of heat down to my toes. Maybe he does want me. With all the teasing and lack of follow-up, the confusion is starting to eat at me. Ask. I should just ask. I make my voice light despite my suddenly pounding heart. "If you are maneuvering to drag me into a bedchamber for the sake of testing Autumn's theory, you should just confess now."

The male stiffens, the sudden hurt flashing in his face almost too quick to catch. "I never confess to anything, lass," he says with a wink. "It's safer for me that way."

I catch Tye's arm before he can pull away, the humor leaving my voice. "What did I say?"

"Nothing."

"Tye." I pause, an unwelcome feeling now burning in the pit of my stomach. "Do you . . . do you not want me that way?" I ask quietly.

He pulls his arm back, his hands going into his pockets. His usually sparkling green eyes are opaque, the angles of his beautiful face carefully expressionless. "If by *that way* you mean as a curiosity or a training aid or a bloody toy, then no, lass. I don't."

My breath catches. I open my mouth to protest but Tye shakes his head. For a split second, I see a whole new male behind the forever-amused mask, a whole life and past that I know nothing about. For a split second, Tye seems all of his five centuries old.

Leaning forward, he brushes a soft kiss over my lips. "We'll know when it's time, lass," he whispers into my ear. "And it isn't just yet." The mask of mischief is back on his face before uncomfortable walking into the supper hall naked, though that little seems a problem at other times, aye?"

My cheeks flush and Tye chuckles softly, running a knuckle across my cheek in a way that sends a blaze of heat down to my toes. Maybe he does want me. With all the teasing and lack of follow-up, the confusion is starting to eat at me. Ask. I should just ask. I make my voice light despite my suddenly pounding heart. "If you are maneuvering to drag me into a bedchamber for the sake of testing Autumn's theory, you should just confess now."

The male stiffens, the sudden hurt flashing in his face almost too quick to catch. "I never confess to anything, lass," he says with a wink. "It's safer for me that way."

I catch Tye's arm before he can pull away, the humor leaving my voice. "What did I say?"

"Nothing."

"Tye." I pause, an unwelcome feeling now burning in the pit of my stomach. "Do you . . . do you not want me that way?" I ask quietly.

He pulls his arm back, his hands going into his pockets. His usually sparkling green eyes are opaque, the angles of his beautiful face carefully expressionless. "If by *that way* you mean as a curiosity or a training aid or a bloody toy, then no, lass. I don't."

My breath catches. I open my mouth to protest but Tye shakes his head. For a split second, I see a whole new male behind the forever-amused mask, a whole life and past that I know nothing about. For a split second, Tye seems all of his five centuries old.

Leaning forward, he brushes a soft kiss over my lips. "We'll know when it's time, lass," he whispers into my ear. "And it isn't just yet." The mask of mischief is back on his face before head. "River can get himself out of this mess. I'm not making excuses for the bastard anymore."

I open my mouth to push her then stop. With my all-encompassing pain lifting, I finally mark the dull, cloudy look in Autumn's eyes, the faint gray bags underneath. I've never seen the female like this before, not even during the intense aftermath of the second trial. "Autumn?" I say, my voice soft, the change of topic clear from my tone. "What is it?"

She looks at me, smiling quickly, though it doesn't reach her eyes. "It's nothing. Just. It's day two now. Kora and her quint have been out for a full night. I thought maybe . . . I don't know what I thought." Her hand goes to the little emerald stud in her ear, twisting it mindlessly. "I'm being silly."

I squeeze her arm, though it's barely a change from the pained death grip I already have on it. "She'll be back," I say firmly. "She has to be back."

AFTER SHADE's intimate healing touches, the Citadel healer's magic feels uncomfortably intrusive. I all but bolt from the infirmary a few hours later, running in to Tye, who I discover waiting by the door.

"Not a fan of healers, lass?" Tye says, a hint of amusement glinting in his green eyes as he gathers me comfortably against his side.

I wrap my hands around my shoulders, snuggling into Tye's pine-and-citrus scent. "I don't know why it feels so different from Shade," I confess before catching myself. Between coupling with Shade and now with Coal, I'm not sure where I stand with Tye.

"Of course it feels different." Tye snorts. "You'd likely feel

ALEX LIDELL

"*Coal.*" She wiggles her eyebrows suggestively. "I can name a dozen females who'd likely come just from seeing the bastard naked."

My cheeks flush a second time, suddenly for a very different reason. Is Autumn possibly one of said dozen? I'm fairly certain the female enjoys both genders but . . .

A corner of her mouth twitches. "You really should do something about that habit of flashing your thoughts for everyone to see. No, silly, I don't think of Coal that way. I mean, I appreciate a good set of everything as much as the next being, but he feels too much like a brother. And when you already have a brother like River, that designation is an incredible turn-off."

I clear my throat, some of the tension easing from my shoulders. "It was . . . good. Different. Intimate in a very . . . explosive way."

"Considering how long it took Coal to put his bedchamber to rights, I imagine that's accurate." Autumn bends to snatch up a flower, twisting the long stem between her fingers. "It's good for him. For both of you."

I rein in my voice to normalcy. "Scientifically speaking, it's fortunate that we discovered the mechanics of Coal's magic in advance of next week. So at least there's that."

Next week. I sigh.

"What's wrong?" Autumn asks quietly, her tone preternaturally perceptive.

"Next week's trial is all River talks to me about now. As if I'm some child whose attention must be focused lest I should wander off and drown in a bathtub."

"River—" Autumn cuts off, folding her arms over her chest. I brace myself for another River-is-the-commander lecture like the one Coal gave me, but Autumn just shakes her

LERA

*O*nce my ribs no longer threaten to puncture a lung each time I take a step—at least for the brief window of time that Coal's magic still simmers in my blood—Autumn walks me to the Citadel's infirmary, a low ivy-covered building near the library. The cheerful blue sky and nodding flowers mock my insides as we make painfully slow progress across the grounds, the clusters of fae we pass watching me unabashedly and whispering the moment we're past.

"Ignore the idiots," Autumn says quietly after the third such encounter, then louder, "They've never trained hard enough to injure themselves."

"If they knew what *training* did this, it might motivate a great deal of study." My cheeks heat when I realize I said the thought out loud. I clear my throat. But the small perk in Autumn's step says it's too late to backtrack.

"So," Autumn says, shooting me a sideways glance. "Coal."

"Coal," I echo flatly.

I can respond, and he pokes my newly healed ribs. "Let's get back to the suite. Autumn was *cleaning* when I left, and if there is a greater sign of trouble than that, I've yet to learn it."

Unfortunately, Tye proves correct, the suite looking disturbingly ordered when we arrive, a gray cloud of tension filling the air.

When, a few hours later, a knock sounds at the door, Autumn sprints to answer it so quickly that she steps on Shade's tail.

The wolf yips his indignation, but when the door opens to reveal Klarissa, and Autumn's body turns to stone, I know no apology will be coming. "Kora?" Autumn's thin voice cuts the air. "Is . . . Are . . . What's happened, Elder?"

14

LERA

"Kora?" Klarissa waves a dismissive hand. "I'm not here about Kora. It's only been a day, and I would little worry about her just yet. I'm here to see—ah, River. There you are."

I feel the large male's steady footsteps behind me, an aura of responsibility filling the air as he steps closer to the door. With a small motion of his wide shoulders, he cuts the line of sight between Klarissa and me. "Yes, Elder?" he says. Low, respectful, and cold enough to chill ice.

"Have you given any more thought to our discussion?" Klarissa asks, her voice as smooth as her champagne elder's robe. They must have had some official Elders Council business today.

"No," River says.

I hold my breath, childishly hoping the elder will argue her point—whatever it is—here and now. Force River's hand into revealing the truth.

"I see." The elder shrugs one delicate shoulder as if she

couldn't care less, but her dark eyes flash with frustration. "Well, that is your prerogative, of course. Now then, I believe it's past time that you fully embraced your status as a Citadel initiate."

Reaching into a hidden pocket in her robe, Klarissa withdraws two envelopes, handing one to River and the other to Tye. "As I'm sure you'll agree, up to this point, the council has been unusually lenient in allowing you freedom to train as you see fit. That ends now. We find the results of your efforts unsatisfactory and will thus be making better use of your quint's time and expertise from now on. The new regimen will benefit all of the Citadel, so I wished to deliver your initial assignments personally. To ensure there was no misunderstanding."

Tye frowns at his envelope. "Was there someone more responsible you intended to address this to, Elder?" He sighs when Klarissa motions for him to read the note, and then his face hardens to stone. A heartbeat later, the paper in his hand flickers with yellow flames. "No."

"Did I say something to imply I was offering a suggestion, trainee?" Klarissa says, her voice never rising from its normal musical alto.

River rips his own dispatch open, his jaw tightening as his gaze cuts from it to Tye. "You shouldn't ask this of him, Elder," River says, so quietly that a chill runs down my spine. "Neither is Leralynn remotely ready." He steps forward, his gorgeous gray eyes locked on Klarissa's dark ones. "If you are unhappy with me, Elder, punish me. Not them."

Klarissa blinks, her face a portrait of confusion. "What in the world are you talking about, River? No one is being punished at all. The simple truth is that, as a trainee, you should never have been allowed to dictate your own training.

We deviated from that, and now the results speak for themselves—the drills you put Leralynn through will not save her from an overzealous puppy, much less the qoru."

Before River can respond, Klarissa turns to Tye. "I expect to see your full effort tomorrow. If I see that you are pulling punches, I will find another instructor for the class. One who might not appreciate the fact that your mortal has a trial to take in seven—no, now *six* days."

"WHAT WAS THAT ALL ABOUT?" I ask after Klarissa leaves in a flurry of silk, followed by Tye, who slams the door in his wake. "And why would you think Klarissa wants to punish you, River?"

River's fist tightens, his eyes not meeting mine. "The council is unhappy with our progress. As the quint's commander, I'm responsible."

Not a lie and yet my chest squeezes uncomfortably at River's words. "What about Tye?"

Autumn rises on her toes to peer at River's note and winces. "I'll explain over dinner. Without the . . ." She throws a dark look at the males, as if it was River, Coal, and Shade's wolf who failed to deliver good news of Kora. "*Them.*"

With no argument from the males—in large part because there is no time for such things, with Autumn lacing her arm through my elbow and striding out the door, iridescent coral silk billowing around her—the two of us find a cozy table beside the enormous tapestry of the fae female playing a harp. Soft evening light streams in through the tall windows, warming my back and making me close my eyes for a moment in blissful, pain-free comfort.

My plate is filled with venison, rice, and a spicy-smelling vegetable medley, Autumn's with three carrots and a stick of celery. Catching my scrutiny of her selection, she gives me a warning glare. "Did you want to know what was in Klarissa's note or not?"

I wisely nod and cut into the venison, letting the female speak at her own pace.

Autumn lays her forearms on the edge of the table. "I obviously only saw River's, but I imagine there is little difference. A bit of waxing eloquent from the council about the swiftly approaching first and third trials, then a reminder that should you fail next week's test, the runes will take your lives—as if River was confused at all about the stakes. Finally—and this is what has Tye upset—the council is ordering him to teach classes for trainees with fire magic. That includes you."

I frown. "That can't be it. Tye trained with me the day before yesterday. And truth be told, I think he enjoyed it."

"He *played* with you the day before yesterday," Autumn said with a wince of sympathy. "Coal is the only one who's ever *trained* with you, and swordplay is a different breed altogether. You are rather unlikely to kill yourself or anyone else with a dull practice blade. Tye works with fire magic, which is about the most dangerous affinity there is, and a very harsh one to train. That male is happy to drive himself into disaster, but he despises making others hurt. Plus, Tye has a self-diagnosed allergy to responsibility."

I frown, chewing over her words. Dangerous, I can understand, but harsh? That word seems as un-Tye-like as a word could get. *And Tye is everything he seems in other ways too, isn't he?* I swallow. "So Klarissa is making Tye teach to torment him?"

"No. I think that's more of a fringe benefit. I really think the council wants him to teach simply because, for once, they can make him do it. Tye is a great deal more skilled than you realize."

"I know our quint is the second most powerful, after the Elders Council," I say. "Or was, before me." I try not to sound bitter at how close to the bone the words cut.

Autumn shakes her head. "Oh, he's bloody powerful. They all are—River especially. But I'm talking about skill. Precision. Before the quint call, Tye was one of Lunos's top flex athletes—that's like acrobatics with magic. It isn't a secret exactly, but Tye never brings it up. I'm truly unsure why, to be honest—it isn't as if he's shy about bragging."

No. He isn't. I twist my braid around my index finger, wondering what sort of game the male is playing. The one I've played into. Who Tye is behind that cocky grin. "Can I ask you something?" Autumn nods and I take a fortifying sip of wine. "Tye always talks about wanting females, but has he ever been shy about, you know, actually making good on his word?" I hold my breath while Autumn finishes chewing, hating to have timed the question so poorly. But at least I asked.

Autumn shakes her head before speaking. "Oh, he makes good on his word. Sometimes he makes good even *before* his word. That one doesn't lack for female company. Ever."

My stomach sinks. So it is something about me.

Autumn frowns. "Has he been playing about?"

"No." For some reason, I'm sure of that. "I was just—never mind." Before I can dissect the thought further, the bell tolls another hour and Autumn flinches, her brilliant gray eyes clouding.

My chest tightens for her. "Is Kora very late now?" I ask

softly, the din of the dining hall a steady backdrop to our low voices.

Autumn rolls her carrots around her plate, her fork herding the little orange logs into a perfect circle. "Technically not. It's been thirty hours. That's about the average time quints take to return, so mathematically speaking, half the quints take longer. Math is just little helping today." She rubs her face. "I didn't think I would care this much until she left, you know? It isn't as if we are . . ."

"I know." I squeeze her hand. "Is there anything we can do?"

"Not unless you have some sway with the council that I don't know about." She stabs a carrot, frowning when it splits apart. "I'm overreacting. Truly. And I was worse when River and his lot went. See, the council had dumped them at a temple near the Mors border and Tye light-fingered one of the artifacts. They were nearly back to the Citadel when River discovered it, and he made them all return to put the damn thing back." She points her fork at me. "Considering that the runes kill any trainee not back at the Citadel within three days, you can imagine the popularity of that particular decision."

"I'd have killed the bastard," I say. "Both of them."

Autumn gives a small chuckle. "You are much better at talking than River is." She pauses. "I need dessert before I can conjure a better compliment. That was admittedly weak."

A follow-up chime sounds before I can respond, and Autumn rises from the table, picking up her unfinished plate. "I should clear the dishes."

I grab the female's wrist, waiting until she meets my eyes. "If there is anything—*anything*—in my power to help Kora, you need only say the word and I'll do it. You have my promise on that."

Her eyes soften. "Thank you, Lera. That helps."

TYE FAILS to return to the suite before I head to bed, snuggling against a warm—if still shedding—wolf. When I rise in the morning, Tye is already gone, the ominous absence making me shiver.

A note brought with the breakfast tray confirms Tye's assignment to teach a class to all Citadel trainees with a fire-magic affinity, which has one Leralynn-the-mortal on its roster. I pull my hair back with a leather thong and straighten my burgundy tunic, breathing courage into my lungs. So long as Tye doesn't repeat that little trick from earlier before a dozen other trainees, I'll get through the morning one way or another.

Coal surveys me from across the room, his gaze lingering on my shoulder.

Obligingly, I move the joint in a circle for his inspection. "You could just ask me how I'm feeling."

"Asking would yield your opinion," Coal answers, his voice calm. "When I watch you move, I get facts."

Right. Well, at least one of us appears back to normal. I push down a pang of jealousy. Just standing beside Coal is making my stomach churn and my thighs press together, neither of which I find helpful just now. Grabbing a sweet roll from the platter, I start for the door. The sooner I'm out of this suite, the better. For many reasons. "I'll see you later," I call over my shoulder. "Tye left without waiting for me this morning, and I'm of a mind to ambush him before class starts."

The chill air outside wakes my skin, the scent of roses from the thorny bushes lining our walkway an uncomfortable reminder of the Citadel's odd duality. Luxury and brutality. Courtesy and control. *A cocky female-obsessed Tye and the real male beneath.*

I shiver, rubbing my hands over my upper arms. A heavy mist cloaks the pathways and lawns of the Citadel grounds, the morning sun having not yet burned it off. The grounds are quiet, only the distant scraping of feet on paving stones echoing faintly off the tall marble buildings.

"Mortal. Wait," Coal says behind me, a few steps bringing him from the door to my side. Hair back in its usual tight bun, the warrior is dressed in a sleeveless black tunic and leather breeches, a long blade strapped along his spine. Stopping a step away, he gazes down at me, his blue eyes brilliant and sharp enough to pierce my chest.

The foot of air between us heats, crackling with an energy that prickles along my skin.

Coal swallows. "I wanted to say . . . I wanted to thank you, mortal." His large, calloused hand reaches for my face, pulling away into a fist without ever making contact. "For—"

I grab Coal's wrist, saving him from finishing his sentence. "Walk me to the practice arena?"

He gives me a grateful nod and starts us into motion, his eyes never stopping their assessment of me. "Don't worry about the chill. You'll be warm enough once training starts."

Right. "So"—I make my voice light—"anything you want to tell me about this training of Tye's?"

Coal puts his hands behind his back, considering the question a great deal longer than I thought he would. "No," he says finally. Several steps later, he adds, "Only that you should not expect to do well."

15

LERA

*C*oal leaves me at the wall of the practice arena and I climb the steps up and the ladder down myself, discovering the round space empty. A horizontal bar is set up in the center, along with several paper targets and a dozen armed crossbows braced on metal stands. The latter point at the horizontal bar as if taking aim, an arrangement that cannot possibly be safe.

I'm about to turn away to look for Tye elsewhere when I realize that the horizontal bar is flexing slightly, as if holding a phantom yet shifting weight. I take a step toward it. A heartbeat later, Tye appears out of thin air, rotates a full circle around the bar, and disappears again.

I jump back, my hand going to my mouth, my heart slowly remembering how to beat. The Gloom. I swallow, watching Tye materialize in midair, release the bar to tumble head over heels, and grip it again with smooth precision before disappearing once more. The male is not only moving in space but also in and out of the Gloom as he does it.

ALEX LIDELL

"Bloody burning stars," a male voice utters behind me. I turn to find a squat, tan male in the orange tunic of Malikai's quint. The male's eyes are riveted to the bar, where Tye now balances upside down, rings of fire encircling him like flaming snakes. "Has someone called the damn circus to town?"

"Aye, Blayne," a second male answers, now joining us on the sand. Tall and willowy, this one has dirty-blond hair and two runes decorating his neck. "And you're invited as its ass. Down!"

I hit the sand just as a flicker of Tye's magic makes the crossbows start firing in a chain, each deadly bolt aiming for the bar where Tye tumbles. My pulse rushes so quickly, the world blinks around me, but Tye never slows, never breaks the dance of power and precision. One arm drops to let a bolt fly past. The other. The male launches himself off the bar, a third bolt piercing the space his head occupied only a heartbeat earlier.

Snap, snap, snap. The release of each crossbow sings through the air, each bolt in turn just missing Tye's perfectly moving body. His bare torso and red hair reflect flashes of his fire, the light and shadow sculpting each perfect, lithe muscle into ethereal, deadly beauty.

A gong sounds through the practice arena just as five crossbows all fire at the same time. Tye spins through a final, gravity-defying sequence and lands directly in their path, a column of flames around him. I twist to see where the arrows hit and come up short.

"Good stars, that isn't a shield," the tall second-trial whispers. "He . . . he incinerated the arrows."

"Of course he did," someone else replies. "Haven't you ever seen a flex tourney, Yalis? That trick's a mandatory element for fire affinities."

"Not at any tourney I've ever seen," Yalis mutters. "They only do it at Realm Championship meets."

Tye's fire dies down, leaving the solitary sound of two hands applauding. "Quite the demonstration, Tye," Klarissa calls musically as she strides across the sand, her golden dress streaming behind her. "Though most instructors prefer to wait until after the students have arrived."

"It was a warm-up, not a demonstration." Tye blinks, his brows rising in mild incredulity as he marks the gathered crowd. As if he'd truly not noticed eight male trainees, two elders, and one mortal until just now. Though shorter than River, Tye still stands above the other trainees, his carved muscles and latent power making some of them look like spindly teenagers. His emerald eyes are all too serious. Dusting a white, chalky powder from his hands, he grabs a gold-colored vest from the base of the horizontal bar and pulls it over his arms. The sleeveless piece hangs open down his chest, leaving his corded arms bare and the smooth skin of his abdomen rippling with each motion. The loose black pants hanging on his hips are the only echoes of the trainee uniform.

"Why is everyone here so early?" Tye's rich voice rumbles through my core. Power, the kind I've not seen rolling off the male before, now burns up all the air in the arena. Judging by the other males' lowered gazes, they sense it too.

"Because we are all eager overachievers," I say, closing the short distance to Tye and poking him hard in the ribs, catching his emerald gaze. I little care what response Tye gives me—a smile, a curse, an insult—so long as I can glimpse my Tye again. Just to make sure he is *my* Tye. My voice drops. "And you scared the hell out of me, I'll have you know."

The male catches my wrist, his grip firm. Not painful, but hard enough to tell me he finds the jest unacceptable. "Fall in line with the others, lass," he says, his eyes already on the nine of us making up the class. On Klarissa in the back, standing with her arms crossed.

I feel cold as I step back, the second-trial Yalis moving over to make room for me. As if I'm suddenly more aligned with him than with my own quint mate.

"Wait," Blayne calls out again, this time stepping forward and taking in both Tye and the trainees with his gaze. "Are we actually here for flex instruction? For stars' sake, someone tell me *why*."

"Don't look at me," Tye says darkly, crossing his arms over his chest. "This wasn't my notion."

"You are here learning flex for two reasons, Blayne," Klarissa says, strolling forward and smiling at the stout male, who has the good sense to blanch. "First, control of body guides control of magic, and flex represents the ultimate mastery of this connection. Second"—Klarissa reaches out and straightens Blayne's collar, her long fingers moving gracefully—"you are here, Blayne, because I ordered you to be here. Fail to perform to your limit, and you can take a rest against the flogging post. Does that help?"

"Yes, Elder. Thank you, ma'am." The apple of Blayne's throat bobs as he swallows.

Klarissa's eyes flow from him to me to Tye, silently making sure we all received the message.

Cold fear clutches my chest and Tye's jaw tightens, his green eyes flashing for a split moment of raw fury before a cool mask snaps into place.

"By demanding simultaneous mastery of both physical and magical power," Elidyr says, walking up to stand beside Tye, "flex allows for feats that would be impossible to achieve using muscle or magic alone." The elder wears black pants and a vest cut in a similar style to Tye's, though his is a shimmering silver fabric instead of gold. His usual long brown braid hangs down his back, the calluses in his wide palms belying his passion for horses. "They are all yours, sir," Elidyr says to Tye, bowing with a mix of respect and suspicious familiarity.

As if the two know each other well. Or did.

Tye nods and straightens his back. "Today we'll be working toward a core exercise in the flex program for fire." His smooth, lilting voice fills the air, sending a shiver down my spine. Replacing the crossbow stands with two targets twenty paces apart, Tye stands directly between them, beneath the horizontal bar. "Elder Elidyr, if you could assist?"

Elidyr, whose magic seems to have an air affinity, snaps his fingers. The targets begin to turn to the rhythm of his snaps, facing Tye then swiveling away a heartbeat later.

Without hesitating, Tye flicks his hands and two small spheres of fire whoosh from him in opposite directions, each striking its target's center.

"This is what we're working toward?" Blayne says, just loudly enough to make ignoring him impossible. "A most effective use of time, to be sure."

Tye turns to the squat male, studying him silently before sighing and stepping out from beneath the horizontal bar. "The sooner you pass this exercise, the sooner we can be rid of each other." He motions for Blayne to take his place between the targets. "All you must do is strike both targets, the right and left, simultaneously. The targets are turning in unison, so releasing your spheres at precisely the same time will be the only way to accomplish this goal."

"What's the catch?" Blayne asks, frowning suspiciously.

"The time limit." Before Blayne can ask what Tye means, a neat wall of fire flares to life in front of Tye and moves steadily toward the trainee. All the while, Elidyr's snaps turn the targets in a steady rhythm, facing Blayne then blading away.

Face. Blade. Face. Blade.

I hold my breath.

On the third swivel, Blayne confidently presses outward with his palms, great flaming spheres shooting from his hands . . . and hitting the wall. He curses. Glances at Tye's approaching flames. Watches the targets.

Face. Blade. Face. Blade.

Blayne's next strike hits only the left target. His third attempt strikes only the right.

By the time Blayne readies himself for a fourth attempt, his chest heaving with the effort, Tye's wall of flames is but a pace away. Spheres of fire fly from the trainee, as if quantity could make up for precision. Except even I can tell that the shots are wild, draining Blayne's power as quickly as he can summon it. Sweat stands out on his brow.

Face. Blade. Face. Blade. The targets keep turning, their pace mockingly steady, though Blayne no longer can spare the time for them. Not as Tye's wall of flame approaches, ready to burn Blayne alive.

I gasp, letting out a relieved breath when a shimmering shield springs up around Blayne, encircling his body just as Tye's fire catches him.

Magic crashes into magic. And shoves.

Another gasp escapes me. I hadn't realized Tye's fire could push as well as burn. By the wide look in Blayne's eyes, neither had he. Now Tye's magic forces the trainee back. One step. Two. More. Until Blayne's back is against the stone wall and the flames surround him in a cocoon.

His scream pierces the air and Tye flinches, even as his fire holds. The scream sounds again, morphing into a choking cough. Only when silence reins does Tye's fire dissipate to reveal Blayne's body, curled up and whimpering on the ground.

I swallow, not knowing where to look. Klarissa strides up to Blayne, the silver shimmer of her healing magic washing over him while Tye returns his attention to the rest of us. As if nothing unexpected took place.

Perhaps nothing unexpected did.

"Simultaneously striking two targets at a wide angle demands flexibility and precision in your magic," Tye tells our silent group. "It's the magical equivalent of doing a split, and until you can do it with your body, you will be unable to perform it with your magic, which must be anchored to your core." Tye lowers himself to the sand, his legs stretched left and right in an impossibly straight line. "Today, therefore, we will work on flexibility. Attempt to anchor your magic to your muscles as you work. Once I feel you are stretched enough to attempt the exercise that Blayne failed, I will let you know. Pair up."

A beat of awkward silence hangs in the air. Casting a long look at Blayne, the other trainees decide to go along with Tye's instructions, sitting with their backs against the arena wall while their partners pull them forward by the hands and simultaneously push their legs outward. In moments, groans of pain fill the air. None chose to work with me.

Left by myself, with neither magic nor partner, I settle to stretch as well. With my legs spread as far as they can go—a shape that resembles a wedge of cheese rather than the line Tye demonstrated—I watch the male I thought I knew walk down the row of trainees, the angles of his beautiful, sharp face in a shape I've never seen before. He goes to every pair, makes corrections to every other being in the arena, before finally stopping in front of me. A stunning, lithe fae warrior, with a mop of red hair and too-serious green eyes.

"I didn't have a partner," I say stupidly.

"I'm your partner." Tye sighs, glances at Klarissa, who stands watch over by the horizontal bar, then crouches in front of me. Close enough that he could brush a hand along my hair, though he does not.

A chill runs through me, Coal's words echoing in my memory. My mouth is dry, my heart racing no matter how many times I tell myself that it's Tye—*Tye*—who sits beside me. "What are we going to do?"

He does touch my cheek then, brushing his thumb across it gently before sitting down with the soles of his boots pressing against the insides of my shins. With my back against the wall and Tye's legs braced to push mine farther apart, there is suddenly no place to go. No escape. Grasping my elbows with his large hands, Tye meets my gaze. "I'm going to hurt you, lass," he says softly. "And it's all right if you need to cry."

16

TYE

Tye was going to kill Klarissa, he decided as he watched Lera sob in pain. He was going to tear the whole damn world apart for making him do this to Lera. For putting the lives and safety of others beneath his care. For making him re-taste a world he'd shut the door on centuries ago.

"Focus on your body; the magic will come later," Tye said, feeling the stream of power she radiated twitch and retreat beneath the strain. It was amazing, truly, to sense her echoing his own power, the feeling of it as palpable to him as his own. The key difference being that Tye enjoyed pushing *his* body to its limits. "Let your muscles yield to the pressure."

The lass was shaking now, thinking herself at a limit that she was still far from. The hitched sobs escaping her throat seared right into Tye's soul.

Tye felt Klarissa's eyes burning into his shoulders. Especially with Elidyr here, the elders would know if he let

Lera off easy—and the retribution would not be pleasant. Klarissa had made that point clear enough.

And the day was already bad enough without that. The mere sight of the familiar equipment, the soft grunts of athletes, the smell of the chalk he'd used to help keep his grip on the bar, flooded Tye with memories he'd worked hard to push away. Made his body thirst for more, even if that *more* was poisoned.

"Tye, stop." Lera's words escaped between desperate pants. Her beautiful fiery brown hair was in wild disarray, some tendrils plastered to her face with sweat. Her creamy skin was blotchy with exertion. The magic was slipping away from her, but her muscles couldn't escape Tye's pressure.

"Easy, lass. Take a breath." He tried to make his voice soothing, the only comfort he had to offer her as, instead of doing as she asked, he pulled her arms further toward him. "It's better if you breathe."

He doubted she could hear him just now, likely busy as she was planning his demise. The worst part of this damn morning was that it was working. Lera's supple curves responded beautifully to his demands, her magic and muscles yielding better than anyone he'd ever worked with. Not that she'd think so.

Lera sobbed silently, her back arching in a fruitless attempt to escape the burning agony. Her body begged for a reprieve, but although Tye could see the words forming and reforming on her lips, they never came. Not because Lera trusted the exercise, but because she no longer trusted *him*. She'd asked once. She knew that he knew her request—and was ignoring it.

Tye's jaw tightened. No one sane ever coached a lover, and this was why. Another minute, Tye decided, and then he'd let her rest while he ran the others through the earlier target exercise. At least two of the remaining seven fae had a chance of passing it.

They didn't pass, though one—the tall second-trial named Yalis—came close on his second try. Yalis now studied the course for a third attempt, a spark of intrigue flashing in his eyes. The trainee was starting to feel the point of it, no longer trying to brute-force the throws and focusing on precision instead.

At least Tye didn't have to punish anyone else the way he'd punished Blayne—there was little need to repeat that point—but all the trainees wore a few burns to show for the attempts. Stars. This was like herding cats. Cats with candles tied to their tails while running through straw.

"I wager that your brute of a trainer would have left you wearing those burns the whole practice, just to deter sloppiness," Elidyr said, coming up to stand beside Tye as he watched Klarissa tend to the latest burn victim—this one having scorched his own thigh.

Tye crossed his arms, his jaw tight. "I was in that training arena by choice. None of them are."

"The quint magic chose them." Elidyr's voice hardened. "Just as it chose you. You are not doing anyone any favors by pretending that fighting the qoru is all stolen wine and dandelions."

"Why are you doing this?" Tye asked, without turning his head. "And don't start on the virtues of flex for a warrior, Eli. These are beginners; the specific magic affinity matters less than basic strength and flexibility at this stage. You could teach this class with your eyes closed—you little need me. Or did you think I'd enjoy this for old times' sake?"

"I'd say your probable lack of enjoyment was more of an

inspiration than a deterrent." Elidyr plucked a blade of hay from his pocket and chewed on the end. "Klarissa wished to remind your quint commander that his choices have consequences. I steer clear of that relationship, but I agree that the weaver needs to be pushed—and your more *enjoyable* methods are likely to lead to a different type of exercise."

Tye snorted in spite of himself.

Elidyr glanced over at him, dropping his voice. "I also had a personal reason for wanting you on a flex field." Taking the blade of hay from his mouth, he turned the dried grass between his thumb and forefinger. "One night, you are Lunos's presumptive champion, readying for Realm finals; you are a legend we whisper about in changing rooms. And by morning, you are in a prison cell, too drunk to stand, much less compete. I want to know why."

"Because I like wine." A chill slipped through Tye, icy dread crackling along his skin until his flesh stung from it. Trust the flex network to find a way to slice him even now, more than three hundred years later. Fine. Shoving Elidyr's words into the same dark place in his mind where the rest of his memories of that time lived, Tye turned his back to the elder and found somewhere else to be. Not a difficult feat in an arena full of beginners trying to kill themselves. By the time Tye had corrected one trainee's form and disciplined another for not watching where his flame snapped, Elidyr had moved away.

At least Klarissa had bowed to Tye's insistence that Lera's training stay contained to flexibility and strength today. Tye suspected that the only reason the lass had stopped crying halfway through the morning was that her tears had simply run out. By the time the midday bell sounded, he was as ready as the trainees to get the hell out.

Standing back, Tye watched the others file out of the arena, Lera trudging painfully beside Blayne. Stopping at the rungs in the stone, Lera stared at them as if regarding a guillotine. A moment later, Blayne—Blayne!—nodded to her in companionable commiseration.

Fire seared everything inside Tye, the world roaring around him. With long strides, he crossed the arena. One glare at Blayne sent the male scampering up the ladder rungs with a reserve of strength that likely surprised Blayne himself. *Good.*

Lera turned, exhaustion twisting every muscle of her body. Even her normally gleaming auburn hair looked tired, escaping her ponytail in errant dull-red tufts. A small cut on her palm had a drop of dried blood on it—from where her nails had dug in during a particularly demanding drill.

"Is there something wrong?" Lera asked, her voice wary.

"Everything is wrong." Tye reached for her, little caring what the other trainees thought of it. What Elidyr and Klarissa thought. No, that wasn't true. He did care. He wanted them to know damn well that Lilac Girl was his and that anyone who stood in his way would burn to ash.

Slipping one arm behind Lera's shoulders and the other beneath her knees, Tye lifted the small female to his chest, her body a soothing, perfect warmth against his. He stepped away from the ladder so others could pass them, and soon they were alone in the arena. Lera's lilac scent filled his nose, even more potent than before. So potent, in fact, that for a heartbeat all Tye could do was stand there, breathing her in and feeling the tired heat from her body spread through his flesh, which woke in more ways than one now that they were close.

Lera frowned, the lines of ache and fatigue somehow making her face even more beautiful. Vulnerable too. And brave. And utterly displeased with him. "What are you doing?"

"I was going to help you up," Tye said, quickly recalculating his plan to rest his cheek atop Lera's head. "You don't have to climb." It was admittedly a small boon to offer her after hours of misery, but Tye had few options just now.

"No." Lera's voice had a bite. "Set me down."

Tye obeyed, his chest tightening as he set the girl on her feet and watched her step toward the wall. He would kill Klarissa the moment he got a chance. For now, however, it was time for damage control. "I'm sorry I did that to you, lass," he said, wondering if he should keep standing or kneel beside her. Picking up the female again was clearly not yet in the cards. "I had little choice in the matter, if that helps."

Ignoring the ladder, Lera slid down to the sand, her back braced against the stone. Her hands curled into fists. "Liar."

"What?" Tye rocked back in surprise. "How—"

Lera's eyes flashed. "You are the one who wouldn't let me do anything, Tye." The words snapped like a whip. "You. Not Elidyr. Not even Klarissa. That bloody female was more on my side than you were."

17

TYE

*T*ye shifted his feet, just to ensure that the world tipping beneath him still existed. The sand was still there, the smell of sweat and lilac. The bit of chalk powder spilling from his pocket. "You are upset because you *didn't* try the split targets?" he clarified.

"Wouldn't you be?" Lera shot back. "Would you be pleased to stretch and exercise in the bloody corner while everyone else . . . Forget it. If we are done training, I'm going home."

"We aren't done." Tye snatched the lass by her upper arms as she tried to rise. Holding her steady, he bent to bring his face level with hers, meeting those large chocolate eyes unflinchingly. "You have neither the strength nor the flexibility to do what you are asking, Lera."

"Neither did anyone but Yalis. You let them try. You let Yalis try three times."

Bloody stars. Tye sighed, his mind starting to hurt as much

as Lera's muscles had earlier. His hands tightened on her arms and he shook her lightly. "Yes, I *made* them try. And they choked for it. Klarissa was healing horrid burns all morning long. You can't even shield yet, lass, and you are mortal. What the bloody stars do you imagine you would have done on that course?"

Lera's eyes glistened, the tears that had not been there for hours now filling her lids. "Discovered why you love it so much, for one."

Tye started, the words hanging in the air between them. He opened his mouth then closed it without speaking, his chest tightening around his heart. He'd just put the lass through hell. She should be celebrating every bit of pain he'd ever endured, and instead . . . Stars take him. He didn't deserve her. None of the quint did.

"One of the males said you were almost the Realm champion, but you never even told me what flex was." Lera wiped her forearm over her face angrily. "And then . . . then you let everyone else peek into your world—everyone except me. I don't care that it hurt; I care that you didn't bloody let me in."

Tye took Lera's face between his hands, her large eyes so full of hurt that he ached to pull her against his chest and hold her there forever. "Lass . . . I . . . ." He had no words. Nothing to say at all.

"You love it, don't you? Whatever it's called," Lera said for him. "I saw it in your eyes when you were flipping. Before we started."

"Flex. Flex-fire, Flex-air, the divisions are separated by magical affinity. And yes, I loved it—though not the pain part. That's Coal's department." A corner of Tye's mouth twitched but settled quickly. He didn't talk about this part of his life, not even with his quint brothers. Not even with Elidyr, who was a bastard but would be most likely to understand. But with Lera . . . It was difficult to deny her that part of himself just now.

Releasing her, Tye crouched back on the sand, his gaze on the horizontal bar still marking the arena's center. "There was a time when flex was the center of my world, Lilac Girl. But that time is long past. As for today . . ." He sighed. "I was trying to protect you. I didn't mean to make you feel isolated. I'm truly sorry for it."

Lera's eyes softened, and to Tye's surprise, she knelt right beside him on the sand and pulled one of his calloused hands into the softness of hers. The leftover chalk on Tye's palm dusted her clothes. "Tell me about flex," she said softly. "What do you like about it? Is there much more to it than the pain?"

Tye chuckled. "It's intoxicating, lass. The rush of flying through the air, defying death, controlling the world." Reading the confusion in Lera's eyes, he grasped for a better explanation. "Most fae feel their magic like a phantom limb and then proceed to wield that limb like a club. Even River, who is powerful enough to make the earth tremble and break, could never slingshot a hundred stones the way top flex-earth athletes can, with each projectile hitting its own perfect target. Of course, River will claim he doesn't need to, that he can just make it rain boulders and let the damn things land as they wish. It's true enough, but River has never felt the thrill of riding the edge of muscle and magic, skimming the impossible. No wine compares to that, lass." *But wine is a great deal cheaper.*

"Why did you stop training?" Lera asked, and it was all Tye could do not to flinch away. "Because of the quint call?"

"No, it was well before that. I quit when I discovered that all games are rigged—whether you play flex or dice. It's just that cheating at flex is a wee bit harder." Tye conjured a cocky smile, a light voice that he knew he'd perfected. "Smart money said I should cheat at dice instead."

Lera's eyes narrowed, that intelligent gaze piercing right through him. Making him feel naked. Tye swallowed, seeking a reason to turn away, even as he knew it was too late.

"You can't really cheat at flex, can you?" she asked. "Not unless you rig the judges or sabotage your opponent."

"Or both." Tye shook himself, his hair flopping over one eye. He'd come to peace with his choices. He had. And even if he hadn't stopped when he did, the quint call would have pulled him from the game just as it had Elidyr. It was stupid to let reality sting him still, after all these centuries. "I'm not the prince of Slait, Lilac Girl. Or even the prince of Blaze. There are some competitions that an athlete of my birth can't win, no matter their skill."

Glancing at the horizontal bar, Tye brushed his thumb along Lera's cheekbone. "You saw the harsh part of flex. Do you think you could hold up a little longer to see its rewards?"

A small, tenuous nod of trust.

Summoning more courage than it should have taken, Tye held his hand out to Lera and walked her to the horizontal bar still standing erect in the middle of the ring. "Grab on," he said, gripping Lera's waist to hoist her up before hopping up himself to hang just behind her. "Just a few more seconds, lass." Releasing one hand, Tye wrapped it around Lera's waist, his legs ensnaring hers like vines. Intrigued at the setup, Tye's magic uncoiled with a purr to twine around him and the lass.

Grinning into Lera's hair, Tye bent at the waist and used their twined legs to start the two of them into an easy swing. Back and forth, back and forth, a pendulum gathering momentum. Waiting until Lera relaxed against him. And once she did, Tye gleefully swung the little minx in a full, gut-clenching circle that made his heart sing as loudly as Lera screamed.

To Tye's delight, Lera allowed him to carry her back to the suite twenty minutes later, keeping her hands wrapped around his neck the entire time. Granted, she couldn't exactly use her arms for much else after this morning's training session. A wicked smile touched Tye's lips. If he played it right, the lass might let him rub out those sore muscles, maybe even hold her for a while.

Truth be told, Tye needed it more than she did.

Still grinning, he opened the door to their suite—only to wish he'd gone elsewhere as angry voices burst forth from the opening.

"You can't let that happen, River!" Autumn's high tone teetered on the edge of desperation, making Tye's arms tighten around Lera.

Stepping in carefully, he found the other males home as well—and keeping a safe distance from the arguing siblings. Opting for the couch, Tye sat himself in the corner, keeping Lera on his lap.

River faced Autumn, speaking too calmly. "There is nothing I can do to stop it, Autumn. You know the runes and magic better than anyone."

"You can go after her. Call for the third trial. The council is willing to leave you in the same location as Kora's quint and then—"

"You talked to the council behind my back?" The ire in

River's voice chilled the air, making Tye's heart beat faster. Canines bared, River advanced on his sister. "How dare—"

"They are in Karnish, River," Autumn said, tripping over the words in a desperate rush. "Klarissa put Kora in the center of a war zone at the Blaze border as bloody bait. To get *you* to move."

18

RIVER

"What happened?" Leralynn's voice sounded behind River, piercing his chest. "River?"

For a moment, her voice was all he could hear, the echo of his name on her lips gripping his spine. He didn't dare turn. Not when he knew that the sight of her on Tye's lap would tear him in two. The sight of both of them.

The glance he'd caught of Leralynn when Tye had carried the female in was enough to reveal puffy eyes and trembling muscles. If the morning was anything like what he'd heard about flex training regimens, the girl had spent hours in agony. As for Tye . . . River's jaw clenched. He didn't know exactly what had happened in Tye's past, why the top athlete in all of Lunos turned into a petty criminal the night before competing for the Realm Championship title. But Tye never spoke of it and his reaction to Klarissa's note made clear that the centuries since that day hadn't healed the wounds. From the haunted look in the male's eyes, the desperate way he held Lera, River knew those wounds now bled.

All of it because River had said no to Klarissa. Because if she could not convince River to take the Slait throne in the name of glory, she'd come at it a different way. If he was refusing power, the female would show him exactly what powerless felt like. River flexed his fingers, using the action to anchor himself to the present reality. And in that reality, Autumn was on a warpath.

River would face the qoru over his sister any day.

Checking his voice, he kept his eyes on Autumn as he answered Leralynn's question. "Kora's quint now has less than twenty-four hours to return to the Citadel," he said evenly. "And my sister believes that Kora has been set up. That Kora's trial was designed to force us into action."

"It isn't just my opinion, River." Autumn crossed her slender arms, the tips of her too-many braids swaying about. "Klarissa all but confirmed it. Or do you imagine it a coincidence that Kora's quint was sent to Karnish, the exact location you refused to go? That the council is suddenly willing to stretch the rules so that you can go to Karnish and see firsthand the havoc that Jawrar's Night Guard is wreaking?"

"It doesn't sound like a coincidence," Coal said, brushing the back of his head warily. "It sounds like an ambush."

"If the council admits that Kora is likely in trouble and they are willing to send someone to aid, why not have a full quint go?" Leralynn asked, forcing River to turn to where Tye held her against him. The male's large hand stroked her thigh with a familiar tenderness that made River's fist tighten in jealousy even as his cock twitched. Leralynn's eyes found River's, her brown gaze suspicious. "It would seem the more prudent approach."

A punch of guilt struck River's gut. Lying to the girl, even by omission, was like dripping poison into his own blood. But he was making the best of bad choices. Leralynn wouldn't understand the trap of Klarissa's demand, the danger that any action against Griorgi would pose to her, without also understanding the history of the king of Slait. And that—the story of how River followed Klarissa's songs of glory until he got his mother murdered—he was not ready to speak of. Even if it made him the coward that Autumn named him.

Autumn's gaze shifted to the girl, making River's spine snap straight. "If saving Kora's life were the goal, then yes," she said bluntly. "But it isn't. The goal is to make River go to Karnish."

Cold silence filled the room, the only sounds coming from the scrape of Tye's calloused hand along the fabric of Leralynn's pants. River's breath stuttered, the questions racing through the girl's eyes spurring his heart into a gallop. A trap. A perfect, stars-damned trap.

River crossed his arms and stepped between Leralynn and his sister, waiting until the latter met his eyes. "You want me to take Leralynn into a Blaze region violent enough to have put a trained quint in mortal danger?" He spoke quietly, slowly, making sure Autumn caught every word.

"You have three hundred years of training, River," Autumn shot back, undeterred. "And Kora has hours to live. I'm asking a warrior of the Citadel to save her life. And you are telling me no because it's too dangerous? Who the hell are you, River? Because you're sure as hell not my brother."

"Don't you dare." River slapped the wall, halting Autumn as she began to turn away. "Don't you dare fault me for trying to keep Leralynn safe."

"You think I'm unaware of what I'm asking?" Autumn said, her voice soft. "That I haven't already thought of all the alternatives beneath the stars."

River drew a deep breath, reminding himself that Autumn didn't know—not really—what it felt like to be responsible for others' deaths. Yes, she grieved for their mother, but it was River who woke up to phantom screams, knowing himself culpable for the murder. Just as he'd been culpable for the death of Shade's twin.

If Autumn knew what that felt like, she'd not be asking him to barter Leralynn's life. His own, yes. But not the girl's.

"I want to go," Leralynn said into the silence. "I want to help."

Of course she did. She always wanted to help, bloody reality be damned. River rubbed a hand over his face.

"River?" Leralynn's voice, so close to him, made him turn. She was pale and standing on wobbly legs, the scent of fear clinging to her neck strong enough to make his fists clench at his sides. Swallowing, she forced up her chin, her warm brown eyes meeting his. "I promised Autumn that if there was anything in my power that could help Kora, I would do it. There were many years where my word was all I had. Please don't make me into a liar."

19

LERA

$\mathcal{W}$e gather in the council chamber, the grand room looking empty with only Klarissa and Elidyr representing the elders. Afternoon light streams through the high windows, glinting off the gilded trim and picking out every detail of the colorful frescoes lining the walls. I feel the echoing depths of fae history in this room, the weight of an old, powerful world that I have only just begun to understand. And barely belong in.

Standing with his arms crossed over his chest, Coal nods to a place beside him, and Tye moves over to create space for me. River's gaze cuts across us all, scurrying so quickly over my face that my chest clenches. Whatever River thinks and feels, he has no intention of sharing it with me.

Plaited hair swaying behind him, Elidyr walks out from behind the dais to stand beside the map of Blaze that River has fastened to an easel. To my surprise, Klarissa does the same. As if we are equals on a single mission. Perhaps, for this short time, we are.

"Are you pleased?" River demands of Klarissa the moment she stops beside him.

So much for being on the same team.

"There is nothing pleasant about the possibility of a quint not returning from the Field Trial," Klarissa replies, smoothing out the folds in her dress. "But yes, I am pleased that you decided to go to Karnish, River." Her eyes flick to me and then return to the male. "Your experienced eye will see the true extent of the danger that the Night Guard poses better than any other."

"And you set up five innocent warriors to make it happen." The chill in River's voice makes my stomach hurt, the gap between us widening with every word he utters. With every secret he keeps from me. A silly little mortal girl who can't be trusted.

The female sighs. "You can't have it both ways, River. Either you take charge and make decisions based on your values, or you step aside and let others do so based on their own priorities. Now, are you prepared to proceed?"

River stares at her for another heartbeat and then, ever so slowly, puts his hands behind his back. "When you are ready, Elders."

I swallow, suppressing a shiver at the odd feel of the room, a professional energy that's too honed to be called tension.

Elidyr steps forward, surveying us for a heartbeat before speaking. "Forty-eight hours ago, Kora and her quint were deposited in a neutral territory near the Blaze border." He points to a spot on the map that makes River nod with comprehension. "As per trial protocol, the females were blindfolded and released in the Gloom within an hour's travel of each other. As the quint has not yet returned, despite all indications that it should have, it is our belief that the females may have strayed into Blaze territory and been captured. The most likely place for such a situation is here, the town of Karnish, where hostile activities have been reported recently."

"When you say 'hostile activities,' do you mean the qoru invading Blaze Court?" I blurt out, not caring how uncouth my interruption may be. Better to sound stupid than discover myself in the middle of a different mess than I think I'm walking into.

River turns to me, his tone too patient. "No. The Night Guard, acting on Emperor Jawrar's orders, is responsible. The qoru themselves have only ever breached the wards closer to the Mors border, and never in numbers great enough to take a whole town."

"River is correct," Klarissa interjects smoothly. "The wards protecting Lunos fortunately still make it impossible for Jawrar to send his soldiers to execute an attack, but he is certainly providing both the funds and the orders to make it happen. Strategically speaking, Karnish is a perfect place to gain a foothold for a future assault, and Jawrar knows it."

My gaze jerks to Klarissa, a feeling that I'm the only one missing some vital piece of this charade sinking through my gut. Likely the same piece that explains why Klarissa cares about River, specifically, going to Karnish. Enough to all but admit to using Kora as bait.

"If our theory is correct," River continues coolly, "then we can expect the Night Guard to have fortified their captured territory and to hold any valuable prisoners they take for questioning."

Stars.

He raises his chin, surveying Coal, Tye, Shade, and me. "As this operation is technically our third trial, it will be constrained by third-trial rules, which limit what information the council may provide and what tools we may bring. Regardless, the mission remains a search-and-rescue operation. By the time we leave here, Kora's quint's runes will be expiring in twenty hours. That is the window available to us. If at the end of this period we do not have the females, the mission will terminate and the priority will shift to us returning home. Nothing else. In either case, arriving back here safely within three days will render our third trial complete. Understood?"

A general murmur of consensus sounds, though I'm certain River's words were primarily for Klarissa's benefit. Still, the female only nods along sagely.

"Yes, no heroics, please," she adds on the heels of River's declaration, one perfectly groomed eyebrow quirked. "If you are unable to retrieve Kora's quint, your priority is to get yourselves back here quickly. I little wish to lose two quints to this mess. Go safely and quickly. There will be time for adventure later. With the successful completion of this mission, you will be one large step closer to leaving the Citadel as a full quint. Meanwhile, I wish to perform one more healing session with Shade before you go. The shifter should be at full strength in case any healing is needed in the field. And after this morning's training session, it would be prudent to check the human as well. You leave in under four hours; get as much food and rest as you can before then."

Without waiting for a response, Klarissa beckons Shade to the back of the room. River crosses the chamber to wait at the door, the hard muscles of his turned back making me flinch. Coal and Tye stay where they are, their tall, calm presences on either side of me keeping my racing heart in check.

Klarissa works on Shade for a quarter hour before clearing him for the trial. When she calls me over to sit in the chair

Shade just vacated, I feel my body stiffen, my joints refusing to bend as I walk closer to the female. Sit down. Take a breath.

Klarissa smiles.

The female's healing magic, efficient and frighteningly powerful, impales me so roughly I gasp, leaning forward and resting my arms on my thighs to catch my breath.

"Are you all right, Leralynn?"

"Yes." Breathe in. Out. "Just taken aback, ma'am."

"Hmm. Yes, with so little time, this is a bit of a brute-force approach. About the opposite of what your friend Tye would call cleanly executed." The female's nose crinkles and her voice lowers to a murmur. "Speaking of the males, a word of caution from one mixed-quint female to another. Tread carefully with River, girl. The prince of Slait is pretty to look at, but he can only ever take you as a plaything. You deserve better."

"I am not River's plaything." The words escape over my better judgment, indignation crowding out common sense.

"You know best, no doubt," the female agrees in a soft, sweet voice. "Though I do wonder why the prince stood by and did nothing during the last trial. Why was it only Shade and Coal who risked their lives when yours was in peril?"

I should have kept my mouth shut. "There was nothing River could do."

"Of course. The prince of Slait thought himself more powerless than an ex-slave and a shifter. It only makes sense." She steps away, leaving my mind a jumbled mess. "You are all set, girl. Go get some rest while we make the necessary preparations."

Tye gathers me against him on our way out, crowding out Shade to claim the space. His hand remains on the small of my back all the way to the suite, even as my mind twists into knots. The warmth of his palm through my tunic reminds me of his powerful flames—and the equally powerful ghosts that crowded the practice arena with him. When this is over, when we get Kora back safe, Tye and I are going to talk.

Tye guides me down the hall toward my bedchamber, the several hours of promised sleep already beckoning to my tired body.

"Leralynn." River's voice hits the back of my head like a bucket of ice water just as Tye and I walk into the room.

Fighting the childish urge to pretend I didn't hear his call, I turn toward him. "Yes?"

River strides into the chamber and closes the door. His jaw is set, his gray eyes an unreadable steel that's as beautiful as it is distant. Impeccably dressed in the wine-colored tunic and black trousers of our uniform, he manages to turn even this practical attire into a badge of crisp perfection. The wide sash wrapped tightly around his taut waist emphasizes the width of his shoulders and the great corded muscles of his thighs. Hands behind his back, the quint commander paces the few steps between the walls. Once. Twice. Five times.

"It's fortunate the floor is stone, not rug," Tye says finally. "If I didn't know better, River, I'd call you at a loss for words."

I furrow my brow, which Tye smooths with his thumb. "Can you just spit it out?" I say finally. "I'm tired and you are making me nervous."

Obediently, River stops in place. Faces me. Lifts his chin. "We are heading into an uncertain situation, likely a combat zone filled with fae warriors of the Night Guard. It is my desire that you have access to as many tools as possible during the mission. Have every advantage that might keep you safe."

"So far, so good," Tye says slowly. "Have you some secret

weapon that she might slip past the runes, or are you here to spout general wisdom?"

"No. Yes." River spreads his shoulders, speaking to me as if Tye wasn't there. "No, I have no way of taking weapons into the third trial with us. However"—his face turns a deep red that creeps up to fill the points of his ears—"if Autumn's supposition is correct, that perhaps there is something to be done to aid you in controlling my power, it could make a significant difference in your defenses. I thought it prudent to try that thing. Or offer you the chance to try it. If you wanted."

"Do you have any idea what he just said?" I ask Tye.

"Aye," Tye growls under his breath before glancing between River and me. "Our fearless leader is offering to lie with you."

LERA

*M*y face heats and it's all I can do not to grab the back of Tye's shirt to keep him from leaving the room. The silence he leaves behind is deafening. Clearing my throat, I brush down my crumpled uniform and conjure the effort needed to look up at River's face. He stands tall and straight, hands clasped behind his back. "You want to lie together?"

River nods curtly. "I only suggest it because it may help you control the magic you echo from me. Magic that may prove vital for protecting you this evening."

I sit on the bed, my legs suddenly giving up on supporting me. "Right now? You want to couple right now?" I sound like a bloody parrot. In my defense, I've never discussed this in such transactional terms. I look at River, his broad shoulders and powerful arms making his beautiful chiseled face even more daunting for his hesitance. "With me?"

River runs a hand through his short, dark hair, a tell of his unease. "It was a rash idea. Forget I—"

"No, wait." I hold up my hand, my mouth dry. The sudden tightness of my thighs alone betrays how much my body wants to lie with River—has longed for it for weeks. As for the rest of me, half of it wants to rip River's cock off, but the other half . . . It wants to lie with River for reasons well beyond aiding my control of his magic. Except I know the male would bolt from the room if I uttered as much. If I told him the truth. "I think it's a good idea. For the sake of safety. And experience. Tonight's experience."

River's shoulders relax. "Yes. For that sake." He steps toward me with his wide, calloused palm outstretched. "It would be a prudent thing for us both to do."

I clench my jaw, swallowing the truth as deep as I can. I believe River loves me, but he isn't *in* love with me. Not like he was with Daz. Stars, I've not met the female and the burrs of jealousy still cut me deep enough to bleed. For all this, River is offering me the one thing he can.

And if I secretly wish to extract more pleasure from it than River's intent warrants, it's only polite to keep that desire to myself.

I brace myself as the male reaches the bed where I'm sitting, his large body shifting the mattress as he sits gingerly on the edge. His gray eyes study me for several heartbeats, straying to where my hands clutch the bedspread to keep from clutching him instead.

The male sighs and reaches forward to brush a stray hair off my forehead, tracing the line from my brow to my cheek to my chin. When the pad of his thumb brushes over my lips, his rough calluses sending tingles of heat through me, I flinch with sudden want. With the need to hide how desperately I long to feel River inside me.

"Are you afraid?" River's voice is a gentle rumble, his gray eyes flashing with that protective instinct that makes River who he is.

Yes, I'm very much afraid. But not of what he thinks I am.

"I . . . I know how it's done," I say, realizing the stupidity of the statement as soon as it exits my mouth. Between Shade and then Coal, there is very little question as to my knowledge of the deed's mechanics.

River kneels on the floor in front of me, letting me look down at him instead of towering over my small form. His fresh, earthy scent fills the air between us. "We need not do this, Leralynn," he says, a gravelly note to his voice. "And if we do, I will go slow. It will . . . I will do my best to ensure it doesn't hurt. To prepare you."

Prepare? Stars, I'm fairly certain that my underthings are damp already. Surely River can smell my arousal.

As if in confirmation, River's eyes flick down to my thighs, then slide to the door through which Tye left moments ago. His jaw tightens. "You had other plans. Do you want me to leave?"

Instead of answering, I take River's hand and move it over my breast, trying hard not to melt into his touch.

River nods once and swallows, his hand tightening gently. When I guide his other hand to my chest, something too quick to read flashes in his gaze. Drawing a sharp breath, River stands up quickly, striding over to latch the door.

"All right then," he says, his broad back still to me as the air's sudden chill brushes away the heat left behind by his touch. Without ceremony, the male starts to undress himself. Boots. The sash hugging his abdomen. The laces of his shirt collar. Reaching behind him, River pulls off his burgundy tunic in a single motion, the chiseled muscles of his back flexing like wings.

141

Stars take me. No one should be able to turn the simple process of taking off a shirt into a sex-clenching ritual, especially without even knowing he's doing it. But it's always been thus with River, hasn't it? Forever there, forever perfect, forever out of my reach. Until now. In some form at least.

I've just realized that I should probably be undressing as well when River reaches for his fly and all thought leaves my head. *Practical,* I tell myself firmly, snatching at reason before it escapes me completely. *This is a practical exercise.*

River turns to face me.

My hands tighten on the edge of the mattress, my body tensing at the sight of his perfect, naked form, a field of muscle narrowing into taut hips and a cock standing erect even now. Yes, of course the male can prepare himself from thoughts alone—more likely than not with memories of Daz.

Heat touches my cheeks as River catches me watching. Likely thinking me an idiot for enjoying the show instead of getting on with things. "Right," I mutter as I rise. Turning my back to him, I reach for my shirt quickly, trying to make up for lost time. We don't have a lot of that. "Sorry."

Attacking the shift first, I pull on the fabric. Once. Twice. *Stars.* Twice my size, my uniform tunic usually feels like a bedsheet—yet the one time I need to remove it expeditiously, the thing grows vines for sleeves, which wrap tighter around my wrists the harder I try to pull them off. My jaw clenches, the humiliation in my throat somehow making my hands work even worse.

I feel River's warmth behind me, his earthy scent and power caressing my skin. Wordlessly, the male takes hold of my hands, calming them. That done, he brushes his wide palms along my body, his touch practical but gentle. Finding the hem, he pulls my tunic over my head with a great deal more grace than I was managing.

Cool air brushes my skin, but I let myself think about none of it as I reach for my chest wrap.

"Why don't I do that," River says, his voice so carefully controlled to conceal reproach that I flush again. "At the rate you're going, you just might strangle yourself with the cloth."

Right. I stand still, begging the stars to open a chasm in the floor beneath me. Instead, they grant me only the efficient feel of River's hands as he removes the rest of my clothes and, sliding his arms beneath me, lifts my naked body onto the bed. Practical. Controlled. Kind. The perfect commander, simply doing his duty to protect his quint.

River hovers over me and runs his gaze down my body, stumbling on my peaked nipples. His breath catches, his hands fisting in the sheets. "I'll—is there anything specific you enjoy to prepare?"

Breathe, I order myself, the proximity of River's body already making me throb with need. Prepare. I think I've been prepared for River from the moment I shared his saddle on our ride through Mystwood—at least my body was. My mind . . . That is another matter. Though thoughts are quickly losing all meaning. Blinking at River, I realize that he still awaits an answer and I feel my sex tingle in spite of itself.

I meet his eyes, the wall inside them too high and thick for me to see through. But as my stomach tightens with hurt, I discover a new desire burning in my core. This coupling, it isn't something River is going to do *to* me. It will be something we do together. Drawing a shallow breath, I run my palms over River's arms, his shoulders. His chest, tight with a held breath as he braces himself over me on outstretched arms.

Tense, hard muscles holding so still for my exploration that

ALEX LIDELL

I wonder whether the male isn't made of stone. Only the sight of his cock, large, glistening, and twitching with every heartbeat, gives away that River is aware of my touch.

In spite of myself, I feel my gaze rivet to the twitches. To the small bead of moisture slipping from the tip of River's cock and snaking down along the velvety head, begging to be lapped off. My own sex, somehow finding the pattern of River's throbs, clenches in an uncomfortable harmony.

Pulling my eyes away from River's cock, I slide my hands along his abdomen, his muscled thighs. Cupping his balls, I stroke the velvet-smooth shaft with my other hand. His eyes shudder closed for one brief moment, then open with a snap as if nothing happened. "Are you ready?" I ask. My voice is hoarse, my lips begging to make contact with his.

"Yes," River says.

Yes. The word echoes through me, filling a longing that I thought would remain a dream forever. Except that in my dream, River said yes for pleasure, not prudence.

I wait for something more from him, for a flash of need or desire. For anything but those neutral gray eyes, that impenetrable wall that will not let me through.

Nothing.

I swallow. "All right, then," I say after a moment, surprised by my steady voice. "I'm ready too."

The male nods and lifts one arm off the bed, spreading open my legs with a warm palm. I whimper softly as my thighs separate with a soft, wet *plop*.

Without another word, River cups my backside, raising it to a perfect angle before slowly sliding himself inside.

144

LERA

I gasp.

The size of him stretching my opening, the sudden fullness inside me, makes my nerves sing. River's eyes flicker, the only sign he gives of feeling anything. He stills at once, giving me time to get used to the length of him. To the girth that still sends a shiver of want through my thoughts.

"Are you all right, Leralynn?" he asks, his voice calm, in control.

No. I'm not. I want to shatter that damn control. For River to move, to grip my shoulders and fill my mouth with his tongue while his cock takes me to the end of pleasure. I want to see the blazing thunder in his eyes. Lifting my head, I brush my lips over his, my heart stilling as I wait for a response.

River tenses, beyond what I already thought possible. When I pull back to study his eyes, I find him staring at the wall above my head. For all the world, I swear he is counting his breaths.

My chest clenches, a stinging bitterness coating my tongue

and eyes. "You can start," I say finally, the words a dull surrender.

With a nod of acknowledgement, River begins to move. A steady and rhythmic *thrust, thrust, thrust* that strikes just right deep inside me. My sex tightens around him, swelling with a zing of need at each impact. My breath quickens, the spot River's cock pounds shouting its agony and pleasure through my core. My hips undulate hungrily, meeting his stroking pelvis, demanding and begging it to do more. Harder. Faster.

Stars. My toes curl, my struggles to rein in my own need doing nothing. *Thrust, thrust, thrust.*

Each plunge of him into me is a surge of sensation, a rising wave that halts a breath short of breaking and recedes for a moment before rising again with the next thrust. My body tightens, my breaths ragged as my legs wrap greedily around River's waist.

He lets out a small choked sound when I lock my ankles, my fingers digging into his trembling arms.

Thrust, thrust, thr—"River!" The name escapes my lips as the deepest thrust yet makes my sex clench like a vice around the male's cock. An unbearable abyss opens inside me, beckoning me closer, each new movement sending a shock wave from my sex to my roaring core. I moan. "Stars. River."

The male's gaze finds my face, his gray eyes glazed. His chest heaves with ragged breaths, his sweat-slicked muscles so bunched, it's a wonder they've not split the skin. River's mouth opens, the beginning of my name forming on his lips, before he jerks his face away, tipping it toward the bloody wall.

Before I can react, before I can think, his hand frees itself to cover my sex. Deft fingers slip through my hot wetness, finding my swollen apex. Circling it once, twice, before grazing it with a single, exquisite stroke that raises a scream from deep inside me.

Sex clamping around River's pulsing cock, I topple over the edge of reason so hard that my body arches, the bed seeming to fall out from under me. As I settle, River's beautiful face constricts with a fierceness that echoes through his body.

Suddenly, another sensation pins my body to the bed as River's magic flares inside him, filling my core with its echo just as his cock fills my sex. I feel heavy with earth, the power within me pushing against River's. The two phantom forces of our magic spin like a pair of dancers across a floor, counterbalancing each other as they twirl faster and faster.

"Leralynn." My name slips from River's lips on a whisper. Warmth fills my chest just as his warmth spills into my belly so wonderfully that I hear myself whimper, only to—

I realize with a gasp that River's hand remains on my sex, his skillful fingers still stroking me despite the release that just racked my body. His magic tugs at mine, demanding that we continue our dance, dive back into that spin that's too fast for either to manage alone. I shudder, yet he strokes me again, ruthless in his resolve.

I writhe beneath him, my swollen bud screaming with the smallest touch of his fingertip. With the aftershocks of pleasure still racking me, I'm too weak, too sensitive to do what River's teasing demands. And yet . . . yet . . . my body responds in spite of itself, my magic rousing alongside my need.

"I can't!" My words are a croak of desire, an exquisite tightness so deep it hurts. "I can't. Not again. Not—"

River pauses, and for the first time since we started, his gray eyes truly penetrate into me. His want, his care, his command, all pierce through me in a single thunder of truth. Holding my gaze, River runs his thumb across my bud one last time and I scream a second release so hard that I can't find my breath.

I'm shaking when River pulls free of me a few moments later, my body so weak and light that I wonder how I don't float away from the bed.

Sitting up beside me, he industriously wraps my shoulders in a warm coverlet, settling me into a cocoon of comfort against the headboard. I wait for the male to say something, to explain that final gaze where our bared souls touched and melded. The one that still burns in my memory.

Reaching out, River brushes a strand of hair from my face, his fingertips lingering on my skin. The scent of earth fills me, the male's heady musk dominating all else in the room. "Leralynn," he whispers again, my name a mere breath on his lips.

My heart stills.

A bell marks the time outside, the sound shattering the silent illusion like a hammer striking glass. River is off the bed at once, sliding into his clothes so quickly that I only manage to get as far as my pants before the male is striding to the door.

"There isn't much time before we go, and you are exhausted," River says over his shoulder, tucking the loose ends of his sash around his waist. "I'll have someone wake you up when it's time to leave."

My world blinks as the door opens and shuts, leaving me alone on one side and River on the other.

I DON'T REMEMBER MAKING it back into bed and falling asleep, but Shade's gentle brush of fingers along my face comes all too soon. Rising quietly—lest my shaking voice give away even more of my nerves than my scent no doubt already does—I dress in the supple leather armor Shade hands me and join the others as we walk back to the elders' chamber.

This time, the whole council is there, standing before their dais. I glance at my males, waiting for . . . something. A hug, a word, a nervous smile. Four calm, experienced warriors look back at me. As if everything that need be said has already been uttered. Probably two hundred or so years ago.

I raise my chin.

"When you are ready," Elder Beynoir intones in the deep voice of a quint commander as he holds out a blindfold.

Shade steps forward, pausing long enough to grip my arm. "When you are left at location in the Gloom, stay put. I'll find you by smell." He gives my arm a final squeeze, his golden eyes steady with command. "Now go to Elder Elidyr."

The three long steps across the chamber's gleaming floors feel like an eternity. My heart hammers, my sweating hands rolled tightly into fists. But I'm not crying. Not even a little. That counts for something.

"Take a deep breath, young one," Elidyr says gently, his hands wrapping a blindfold around my eyes. Despite my pounding pulse, the male's smell of hay and horses, together with his calm voice, adds a measure of comfort. "I'm going to bring you through the Gloom to your trial site. Have you moved through folds before? They let us travel greater distances more quickly. A corridor of sorts."

I nod, remembering the passage Autumn once used to bring me from Slait's border into the palace.

"Excellent." Elidyr sounds pleased. "We will be making use of several of these on our way to the destination. You are unable to step into the Gloom yourself?"

I nod again, proud that my muscles are not shaking.

A solid hand presses between my shoulder blades. "That is not a problem. I will take your hand now and we will step together, all right? I'd like a verbal response, please."

I lick my lips. "Yes, sir."

"I've not taken a single third-trial who was not petrified, Leralynn. That has not stopped most of them from returning."

I think he means the latter to be comforting, but the words utterly miss their mark. Not that it matters, since a moment later, I feel Elidyr pull me along into the darkness. A deep chill penetrates my bones. The male guides me in blindfolded silence for what seems like an hour, though I doubt it is really that long. By the time we stop, I'm certain I've left bruises on his skin where I gripped his forearm.

I smell dust, damp. Metal.

"Here we are," Elidyr informs me finally, his voice sounding distant though he stands right beside me. "Count to ten before removing the blindfold. You have seventy-two hours to return. Good luck."

22

LERA

"Wait!" I call into the cold silence. My body tenses, my mouth drying even as my hands open and shut with a sudden influx of blood. Even without seeing, I can feel the Gloom's gray oppression saturating the air.

No answer.

I rip off the blindfold. To hell with counting. I am in what looks like a basement, one narrow streak of light illuminating the dim space. The room around me is square, the stone walls covered with bits of glowing blue moss. A pile of loose metal and wood scraps makes a mess in one corner of the room, though the large empty worktable beside them is clear. I wonder what's missing, what would be here in the Light—how some objects exist here and others do not.

Regardless, I need to get aboveground. Connect with the others. Shade has promised to find me by scent, but it will be faster if I'm in the open air. And even if it weren't, the notion of staying here, in this underground tomb, sends a cold sweat along my sides.

Stopping by the pile of junk, I quickly flip through it in search of anything weapon-worthy, since "bring no weapons" is one of the brilliant third-trial rules. Coming up with a rusty old sword, I tuck it into the back of my sash. Better than nothing.

Seeing no staircase up, I walk the perimeter of the room in search of a door. Nothing. I curse. The door and stairs, which no doubt exist, never made it into the Gloom. If I could maneuver between the Gloom and Light, I might step out and try to use the resources that way. Although, in the Light, there might be fae occupying the house. Ones who might or might not welcome a stranger. Just now, I'm rather grateful that most of Lunos's residents either can't or won't step into the Gloom.

Following that small stream of sunlight, I find a narrow, horizontal window near the ceiling. Metal bars cover the opening, but I'm likely small enough to fit between them. Thank the stars. Now, to get there. Tye could no doubt simply jump, grab the ledge, and pull himself up without wasting a breath. For me, however, it would be a climb. I run my hands over the rough walls in search of holds, finding few nooks worth the title. Wiping my moist palms on my pants, I grasp the tiny seams, the toes of my boots turning stone nubs into footholds, and pull myself up.

My hands slide off at once, the momentum I used to propel myself up pulling me back instead. Losing all balance, I fall backward. The ground rushes up to slam into me, the thud of my fall dulled by the Gloom's oddness. The sword tucked into my sash leaves a deep ache along my lower back.

Damn. Taking a moment to force moldy air back into my empty lungs, I rise to try again, the lack of grips and holds laughing at me as I approach the wall. I glance at the worktable, too heavy for me to move, and briefly wonder whether I might jump from it to the window ledge. I could—if my goal were to break a leg instead of escape.

The wall it is. Gritting my teeth, I reach for the pitifully small holds, this time making it two steps up before falling back to the packed-dirt floor.

A whimper escapes my throat, the walls closing in around me, the basement now a crypt marooning me alive. My heart quickens, my breaths growing shallow with panic. Dark and cold and stone. A trap with no escape. No air.

Coal. I make my breaths slow. The fear of the small space is Coal's, not mine. Or *was* Coal's. Apparently he shared. I force myself to stand, my legs shaking. Coal escaped a much worse cell than this pitiful little basement, didn't he?

Walking up to the wall for the third time, I plan my route before heading up. Find every crevice before stepping up again, my fingers straining with the effort of holding me to the stone. Legs. I need to use my legs—push up, not pull up. That's what Tye told me during training. I press my hips close to the stone, feeling my balance shift. *Better.*

My right toe finds a sad excuse for a hold and I dig into it, pushing my weight onto my leg while only my fingers keep me anchored to the wall. Left foot. Right again. I realize I've been holding my breath only when my hands clasp the window ledge. My leg slips. Catches against the opposite wall, stretching me painfully. I push up with a final heave that sets my knee on the ledge, and I grip one of the metal bars.

I stay still for a moment, relief flooding my body, and then I kneel. Taking the sword from the back of my sash, I go to break the window but discover that the glass hasn't made it into the Gloom. Small fortune. Tossing the sword through the opening first, I slide after it, the slit between the window bars barely large enough for my small frame.

One long scrape along my spine later, I am outside on all fours, gasping for air. A thin streak of pain burns my back, but I little care. If I never see another cellar again for the rest of my life, it will be too soon. Shaking myself free of that thought, I survey my new world. A ghost of a town main street, if the road's generous width and the three-story stone buildings lining its sides are any indication. My jaw tightens.

The understanding was for us to be dropped in the same locations as Kora's quint, though the elders could not reveal exactly where each of us would land without negating trial rules. Yet this little looks like the neutral territory that Kora's quint is believed to have wandered away from. It looks like a well-built town. A mining town. Either the elders lied about where they dropped Kora, or they lied about where they would drop us. *And what did you expect exactly?*

I return my attention to what can only be Karnish.

A shiver runs through me at the emptiness, the dull echo of what I imagine is a vibrant place in the Light. Or perhaps not. Most fae might lack the ability and interest to step into the Gloom, but if what Klarissa said about the attacks is true, then Karnish's inhabitants might not be here in the Light either.

I start down the street, looking for a good place to settle. The sun should be setting here within the next couple hours, but in the eerie twilit grayness, I'm not sure I'll even notice the difference. The Gloom muffles my steps, washing the world of colors and smells. Green grass is a muddy brown; the trunks of stout, neatly manicured trees that line the street are a tarnished black; the wooden signs are shades of listless gray. One sign that looks to be advertising a mercantile swings in its frame with a dull, eerie creak, though I can't feel the breeze that moves it. Spotting stacks of firewood beside what must be an inn, I decide to set my nest there. Crossing the street as if moving through a fog, I've just reached the wood piles when a familiar stench of rotten meat hits my nose.

Sclices. My heart stutters and pounds against my ribs, memories of salivating fangs and hog-like snouts racing through me. Ducking quickly behind the wood, I pull my shirt over my mouth and nose to muffle the stench of Mors's rodents. Bloody stars, first the tomb of a room I woke in and now this. Will the sclices' smell throw Shade off my scent? Or worse, will my own attract the beasts right to me? My hand closes stupidly around my rusty sword. I don't think I can hold my own against a single sclice, and the rodents usually travel in packs.

Upwind. Yes, I should move upwind. If nothing else, it will give me something to work toward instead of sitting here, stewing in terror.

Peeking out from between the stacks, I survey the street, looking for movement. Nothing. Even the tattered Blaze flag hangs limply from its pole. I've just located a new hiding place in a lean-to structure twenty paces away when a shadow falls over the road. I hunch back down, holding my breath as I peer between the chucks of firewood.

The shadow moves, still too rough to hint at who—or what —is casting it. A sclice beast? One of the mercenaries patrolling the Gloom? Surely my males would be more careful than this. The shadow hesitates then quickens, its owner finally stepping into my line of sight.

Blood drains from my face. My heart gallops, my breath caught in painfully stretched lungs. No. Impossible. It can't be. And yet . . . yet there it is. Webbed hind legs. Leathery gray skin. Standing upright. An expressionless cave of a face with a round maw of needle-sharp teeth pointing in all directions. The beast from Coal's nightmares—a qoru. Here in Lunos, despite everything River and the council and all the males said.

The qoru disappears into a large stone building with a bubbling ale stein on its sign, what I presume to be a saloon.

Something scratches behind me. I jump, a scream forming in the back of my throat just as a large, calloused hand clamps over my face. I sink my teeth into it, bucking against the muscular body suddenly pressed against my back.

23

LERA

"*E*asy, lass." Tye's soft voice in my ear is too smooth for the reality of the street. His scent of pine and citrus slowly soothes my instincts even as my muscles still tremble. "All right now?"

No. No no no.

Tye releases my mouth, his arms wrapping protectively around me. "Didn't Shade tell you to stay where you were dropped?"

"I . . ." I swallow. "It was a basement and there was no escape, so——"

"It's all right." Tye's arms tighten, the warmth of his body anchoring me to sanity. "I'd take you into the Light, lass, but the place is crawling with the Night Guard. Can you manage the Gloom a bit longer?"

I nod shakily, pulling my mind together. Search and rescue, that's why we are here. And the rescue is of Kora, not me. "There's a qoru here," I say, reaching for the cool voice that

Tye used in the practice arena. "Down at the other end of the street. And I'm sure you've smelled the sclices too."

"You recognized a qoru?" Tye says, his brow lifting in question. I've not exactly told him about seeing into Coal's nightmares, and I doubt the warrior has volunteered the information. "From Coal." Tye works out the answer to his question, his face grim. "Qoru being here shouldn't be possible —we are too far from the Mors border."

I know the words are coming—*you must have made a mistake, lass*—but my chest tightens in anticipation nonetheless. Tye doesn't believe me. Though I understand why he'd doubt my assertion, it still hurts.

Tye shakes his head, his shaggy red hair flipping into his eyes. "Bloody academics and their bloody theories. Next time they want me to read some book, I'm reminding them of this. All right. Where?"

A spark of warmth loosens my chest and I point to a stone building at the end of the street. "The one with the rainbow-shaped signpost and the picture of an ale stein. Do you think the qoru captured Kora's quint?" Captured. Killed, most likely. "We need to check."

"We need to keep you alive." Tye pulls me behind him. "Where the bloody hell is Shade?"

As if summoned by the name, a wolf trots around the corner, his muzzle drenched in rust-colored blood. Clearly, I was not wrong about the sclices. Seeing me, the wolf's yellow eyes flash and he leaps forward, two hundred pounds of muscle pressing into me so hard that I fall backward, caught only by Tye's strong arm. A warm, wet nose snuffles into my hand, followed by a low, nearly inaudible whine.

"I missed you too, Shade," I say, rubbing the soft gray fur on his head.

"Can we all snuggle later?" Tye says. "Not that I blame you, lass, with the likes of us around."

I roll my eyes, opening my mouth to offer a retort just as Tye clamps his hand over it again, this time pulling me down to the ground.

His lips press against my ear, his words a soft, warm brush of air. "Someone is coming."

A few moments later, I hear the voices myself.

". . . harvest what else they know," a fae male says. "And make our honored guests aware that their meat will expire in half a day. Unless they feed now, there may not be another offering for a while."

I grab Tye's shoulder so hard that I know it must hurt.

"They don't eat the meat," another male answers, his voice younger and more nasal. "They suck the life energy through— ow! Sorry, sir."

"Any other wisdom you wish to share, Jik?" the older male demands, his deep voice quite unamused.

"No, sir."

"Then be about it. And be sure to return to the Light before too long." The voice gets louder, as if the two are separating. "That you *can* roam the Gloom does not mean you *should*. It drains you, no matter how strong you are."

I wait until the sounds die away and Tye's hand between my shoulder blades eases. When I turn my head to suggest we follow Jik, I find Shade's wolf sniffing a piece of fabric that Tye pulls from his pocket, the animal's ears perked up to attention. Tye's other hand pushes a few stones into a small pile.

"Kora's scent and a marker for the others," Tye whispers, unabashedly drawing the rusty sword from my sash and keeping it for himself. "We've done this before a time or two, Lilac Girl. Get ready to move."

Pushing past me, Shade's wolf scouts ahead, his lithe form slinking through the eerily empty streets. Tye and I follow, our progress made of short hops from the back of one building to another, stepping lightly on the dull gray paving stones. The air smells like dirt, coal—a mining town—with something disturbing just under the surface. A faint whiff of rot carrying on the breeze. Tye's sharp face is tense, his clear green eyes surveying every shadow, every seemingly abandoned building. Every time we stop, while Shade trots on to get a scent, Tye builds that small marker of his. Twice, his strong arms flatten me to the ground, his preternatural senses aware of the prowling sclices—or whatever else is here.

The third time he pulls me down—this time behind a tall wooden fence at the back of a building, closer to the qoru's saloon than I'd like—I discover River and Coal waiting there already. The moment I see them, something releases in my chest, some tightness I've been carrying ever since we were all separated. I touch them compulsively, River's hard shoulder, Coal's warm chest. They're here. We're all here, together, where we should always be.

"Any problems?" River asks, his eyes—like Coal's—drilling into me, checking every bit of flesh. "Besides the fact that we are now officially violating Blaze's neutrality and should be executed?"

"The Light is crawling with the Night Guard and the Gloom has at least one qoru," Tye says softly. "Our package is likely alive, being held for feeding."

My stomach turns but I force my spine to straighten. This is good news, I remind myself. It's the reason we came. I point to a building two doors down from us, its back alley a jumble of ale barrels, wooden pallets, and empty sacks. "I saw the qoru entering the saloon, there," I say, trying to sound as steady as the males. "Do you think it was heading to dinner?"

River nods. "Let us ruin its appetite. Leralynn, you—" River pauses, his gray eyes piercing mine before he finishes his sentence.

Don't leave me behind. Don't leave me alone. Don't leave me behind. Don't leave me alone.

"You stay between Coal and Tye as we move, understand?" River says.

I nod, ridiculous relief mixing with the fear.

Coal reaches for me, his metallic musk filled with calm strength as he brushes his hands along my clothes, tucking in loose pieces of fabric and muffling a belt buckle that I hadn't realized made noise. That done, he performs a similar inspection of Tye and River, though no adjustments are required in their case. I know him well enough by now to see the tension riding under his gaze. He's not as calm as he lets on—he never is.

"I checked out that building on my way here," Coal says as he works. "There is a back window suitable for entry. If there is a qoru here, he'll want to be beneath ground. Even in the Gloom, that is their preferred habitat, especially for feeding."

Right. Of course. Glorious.

Following Coal, we move stealthily toward the saloon and line up outside a back window similar to the one I climbed through earlier, though this one is fortunately without bars. With Shade at the front of the stack and Tye bringing up the rear, the males push close enough to feel each other. A team. A unit. Despite my unease, a trickle of excitement runs through me, twining with a bewildering sense of belonging. We aren't in the practice arena any longer, but the residue of training

161

must be clinging to me somehow. Maybe even enough to do some good.

A hard hand squeezes my shoulder and it takes me a moment to realize that Tye intends for me to pass the squeeze forward. I obediently press Coal's bicep in my palm. He passes it on to River. With one more heartbeat, we move in.

24

LERA

*S*hade enters first, his body a streak of gray as he flies through the air with muscled, lupine grace. A moment later, a short yip sounds and River drops through the window, followed by Coal. Tye hands me down to Coal without a word, then climbs inside with a controlled grace that I remember well from the practice arena.

Looking around, I see further evidence that we've entered a saloon. The cellar around us is filled with barrels and grain sacks, tap handles and chairs too broken to be of use in the main room upstairs, and stacks of firewood and cleaning supplies. A staircase leads up to an opening in the ceiling, currently covered with a hinged door.

I frown, realizing that the room we stand in is much too small to be the full basement of the large building above—and yet, bar the pull-down exit by the ceiling, I see no doors or corridors leading from the space.

Shade's nose points toward the far wall, hackles up, tail swaying like a pendulum. Right, left. Right, left. The wolf's upper lip curls back to show glistening canines, which manage to reflect what passes for sunlight here.

"Trapdoor," Tye whispers into my ear. "And our package likely behind it."

Before we can move forward to confirm Shade's prediction, the *click, click, click* of steps echoes from above us, the hinges of the ceiling door screeching their discontent. My heart stops. The door begins to open. My body wants to freeze but instinct has me ducking and sliding silently behind the piled grain sacks instead.

The others are there already, as calm as if sitting in our suite's common room. Coal gives me a nod then finds River's face, his hands flashing in quick motions, one of which draws a line across his throat.

River shakes his head.

"It's past time," a hissing voice says, the scent of rotten flesh throwing me back into Coal's memories. A small shake comes over my body as the *click, click, click* starts up again, skittering down the steps. The qoru. Here. Even having seen one of them on the street, the knowledge that I'm sharing this building with one makes bile rise into my throat. Through a small crack between the grain sacks, I catch mottled gray legs heading for the wall that Shade just alerted us to. A second pair of legs. A third.

A long-fingered gray hand reaches for what must be a latch, because a moment later a whole slab of stone wall slides away on soundless hinges. One, two, three sets of legs disappear into the new opening.

A brief moment passes.

"Now." River's quiet order has the males moving right before Kora's screams confirm our suspicions. Shade, Coal, and River vault over the grain sacks and rush silently for the door, Tye staying back to cover me.

When Tye's hand grips my shoulder, I realize his magic is awake and engaged. Ready. A phantom thread of magic wakes inside me as well, crawling through my veins like a stretching tiger, the sensation leaving me both more secure and more vulnerable. *Don't touch it,* I repeat to myself firmly. *No bonfires in a cellar. Leave the tiger alone.*

By the time Tye and I reach the hidden room, bodies face off in the dim light with grunts and clashes of swords, and the floor vibrates with River's magic. I gasp as that too stirs in my blood, the coupling clearly having enhanced my ability to feel River's power. Fortunately, he stops before the new sensation overwhelms me completely, and I can once more pay mind to my surroundings.

We are in a large room, its walls stone, its floor made of packed dirt soaked with blood and piss. Tiny slits along the ceiling provide slivers of light, showing Kora's four quint mates chained to the wall. I stare at a fifth, empty set of shackles, my guts twisting as I turn to find Kora held in one of the qoru's arms, the thing's sharp teeth buried in a spot at the back of her neck, seemingly oblivious to the mayhem around it.

Coal is already moving toward it, a sword he obtained somewhere taking the feeding qoru's head cleanly off its shoulders. Even as the detached body falls away, the qoru's teeth cling to the back of Kora's neck.

The female falls to her knees and pulls the qoru's head off her with a panicked gasp, the skin around the wound a bloodless white-gray blotch.

River and Shade, the latter still in wolf form, square off against the two remaining qoru, while Tye turns to cover the door in case we've more visitors. I rush to Kora, sliding an arm around her quivering shoulders, brushing her ice-cold skin. Her green uniform is tattered, stained, barely recognizable. Her normally bright-blue eyes are dazed and bloodshot. "It's all right. Look at me, Kora. You're safe now."

The clashing bodies and swords, the cries of pain and fury, are a blur around me. I focus only on helping Kora, fueled by Autumn's wide gray eyes and panicked voice. We must not fail.

"You wouldn't happen to have keys, would you?" Tye calls, darting a glance at Kora over his shoulder. "We need to free the others."

Kora grabs my hand, her grip soul-wrenchingly weak. "You need to leave," she says, her words coming raspily from a throat that's clearly been screaming. "You need to leave. You can't be here."

I put my hands on either side of Kora's face, forcing her blue eyes to meet mine. "You are safe now," I repeat, the words tightening my chest. Despite everything, I'm *glad* to be here. To be doing something worthwhile. My voice strengthens. "We are going to get you and your quint out of here, Kora. We're going home."

Kora jerks away from me, reaching a pale arm toward River—who, having disposed of his opponent, now examines the prisoners' shackles. "You need to leave, River—*now*. You are too valuable. If they capture you . . ." Now that she says it, I see the echo of her words reflected in all the females' flesh. They weren't kept here only as an afternoon snack; they were questioned.

"Not now, Kora," River says soothingly, still examining the others' shackles. "We're going to get you out of here, and then you can tell us everything."

Kora groans, panic in the whites of her eyes. "You're not

listening to me. There are several dozen qoru here," she says, speaking quickly. "I don't know how they got into Lunos, but something has been breached. They spoke of a gate. Something opened from *Lunos's* side, not Mors's. The Citadel needs to know. Between the qoru and the Night Guard, they've killed what's left of the village in the Light. They—"

"They control the Light and the Gloom, both," an unfamiliar voice says. My stomach turns. Around us, fifteen fae warriors—three quints of the Night Guard—step out of thin air. All of them, males dressed in black with blood-red accents, are grinning and armed.

Swords and crossbows pointing at us, the fifteen warriors herd us into the center of the room, just as a small pack of qoru stride in behind them.

The middle of the qoru looks larger than the others, his lidless eyes a deep shade of red with specks of rust. Unlike his scantily dressed entourage, this qoru wears a sash across his shoulder, the supple leather decorated with jewels so fine they manage to sparkle even in the Gloom. He turns to Coal. "Well, what a reunion." His voice is like the low creak of a rusty gate opening in the dead of night. "Have you nothing to say to your emperor, buck?"

Emperor? My blood freezes. *Emperor Jawrar.*

The qoru's attention shifts to River, his round mouth widening slowly into what must pass for a smile. "Jik." Emperor Jawrar snaps his fingers at one of the Night Guard males. "Fetch Griorgi. Tell him his son has come for dinner."

25

LERA

on? King Griorgi—River's father—is here. Working with . . . with Emperor Jawrar? Is that how the qoru are here, beyond the wards meant to keep them in Mors?

Lies. Qoru lies. They have to be. I look at River, my throat closing as I see Jawrar's words drain all the blood from the commander's beautiful face. Not a lie. Truth. Stars. I long to reach out to the warrior. But there is no reaching out. There is nothing.

I am too dry-mouthed to scream as two sets of Night Guard hands grab me, dropping me hard to my knees. My bones yell at the abuse and my body fights to react, Tye's power still bubbling in my veins. Fire. I could—

I catch Tye's head-shake as he too is forced to the ground. An order to stay put.

He's right. I would only set the cellar aflame and cook us all like so much steamed meat. Plus, he'd have already done something if he thought it would work. Instead, Tye kneels on the ground just as River and Coal do. Shade's wolf is

169

ALEX LIDELL

held at bay with a crossbow, a guard's belt wrapped around his black muzzle. I draw a ragged breath, the sight of my males not fighting sending the coldest chill yet down my spine.

The emperor turns to the pair of guards holding Coal. "Chain that one up. I've a few who would be pleased to reunite with the buck . . . personally."

The deafening sound of shackles closing around Coal's wrists echoes through the room. Coal's face is stone, his blue eyes an unbreakable mask that gives away nothing of the nightmare he's living through.

Jawrar surveys our quint, hesitating on me and stepping closer. Bile rises up my throat as he approaches, filling my mouth. A hand so gray it reeks of rot reaches for my face, and I pull uselessly against the night guardsmen holding me in place. No. *No.*

"No!" Coal roars. Not at Jawrar, I realize, but at River.

Too late. A shock of power booms through the room, shaking the ground so hard that it's a wonder the walls still stand.

Jawrar pulls back from my face, a shield as black as darkest night flashing around him. Whatever burst of power River launched is swallowed silently into darkness.

Slowly, carefully, the qoru twists toward River. Jawrar's leathery gray hand rises. Slashes down.

River doesn't scream, but I do as I see the skin on his cheek pull away from his flesh, splitting into a whip-like gash. River jerks against his guards' hold, his jaw tight. Another stripe appears, this one on his neck, spraying his shirt with blood. A third, on his back. A fourth. The fifth strike of Jawrar's invisible whip finally draws a grunt of pain from River's shaking form.

170

"Muffle it," Jawrar orders the night guardsmen holding River. "I can't hear above the noise."

Turning his attention right back to me, the qoru's slitted nostrils expand. "The female smells wrong," he calls to someone in the cellar behind him. "This little filly has no blood of yours, Griorgi. Not even of fae."

"Of course not," answers a low voice, its deep sophistication hauntingly familiar. A corruption of a voice that I know and hold dear. Its owner enters the room a few heartbeats later. As large and dark-haired as River, with shoulders wide enough for two males, King Griorgi wears an intricate tunic of brown leather studded with rubies. Harsh and gaudy. Like River, Griorgi steals all the air from the room, but through a toxic presence rather than a commanding one. The strong planes of his face echo River's, but his nose comes to a hook that turns him from handsome to hawkish. Eerily familiar gray eyes skip over River—who's biting back screams through the gag stuffed into his mouth—to rest on Jawrar. "Autumn is not part of this little nonsense. Let me speak to my pup."

The night guardsmen holding River pull the gag from his mouth, though the invisible lashes continue to mark his shirt with blood.

River gasps for breath, spitting blood to the floor as he straightens his back. His chin rises, pain hidden behind his blazing gray eyes. "What are you about, Father? Working with Jawrar? Have you lost all sense?"

"And you wondered why I didn't choose him as my emissary," Griorgi calls over his shoulder to Jawrar, before returning his gaze to River. "Is this truly what you've come to, son? Scurrying about the Gloom like a foot soldier? Mingling with sniveling mortals? Tell me, does Klarissa clip a leash on

171

you when you are back at the Citadel? Do you still enjoy following after her like a lost pup, pissing on walls at her command?"

My breath catches, River's utter lack of emotion burning my heart. He knew. Not that Griorgi was here, working with Jawrar, but what his father was. Is. What Griorgi thinks of his son. A critical, soul-wrenching piece of River's world that he's kept from me. Just like he once tried to conceal his royal lineage from me altogether.

The knowledge that River never truly trusted me hurts as badly as watching him bleed.

Griorgi strides forward and squats before his son, his strong features twisted into a cold frown. "The world is changing, River. Lunos is changing. This reveal might be a bit ahead of schedule, but truth is truth. The qoru are coming out of Mors into a new world. One where Lunos and Mors are allies. Trading partners."

"With you in charge of Lunos?" River says, viscous blood now dripping to the floor beneath him, the new wounds not even appearing through his soaked shirt.

"Of course," Griorgi says simply.

"And when Jawrar decides to drain you and leave your husk to rot?" River says. "What happens then?"

Griorgi sighs, shaking his head. "Stop letting your own fear cloud your senses, boy. A good alliance isn't built on trust; it is built on checks and balances and contingencies. My death would stop the good emperor here from being able to travel to Lunos, and that is something neither of us would find convenient." Griorgi's voice changes. Becomes deeper, more dominating than even Jawrar's. "You are still my blood, River. My flesh. Join me, and I will welcome you back."

"Go to hell," River growls.

Griorgi rises, shaking his head. "Idiot, but still mine," he tells Jawrar over his shoulder. "I want to keep him. If nothing else, it will bring the other one trotting in. Sooner than I'd have liked, but flexibility is a virtue."

The other one. Autumn, who's in charge of Slait Court's Gloom patrols.

"Do you truly need the girl's assistance?" Jawrar asks, a hint of exasperation entering his voice. "If those patrols are so bloody loyal to her, just scorch the Gloom and be done with it. I little like the extra moving parts."

Griorgi crosses his arms and shrugs, his ruby-studded armor moving gracefully. "I could. I choose not to." A hint of a smile. "My intent is not to let you roam free throughout Slait, Jawrar, which is what your request would accomplish, but to bring the rogue elements under my control. Dead warriors do very little for me."

"I'll get you new warriors," Jawrar says with a snort.

"No doubt." Griorgi smiles in earnest, the intelligent glint in his gray eyes so like Autumn's that my breath catches. "However, I will make the decisions about my court. I'm certain you understand." Not an idiot. Whatever else the bastard is, he unfortunately is not an idiot. "River lives," Griorgi continues. "You may kill the others. Feed on them if you wish, or have them disposed of outright. I little need the extra bodies around. This isn't a—"

"Meat market?" Jawrar's lipless face twitches in what I can only assume is a smirk. "Debatable. However, yes, I do take your meaning. There has been too much playing with food as it is. The mortal and that buck over there, I want to speak with personally. The rest, we'll have taken care of in a few hours."

26

LERA

"Wait!" I don't realize I'm speaking until my own voice fills the room. The sudden silence, punctuated by River's quiet grunts of pain, presses on me from all sides. My heart races, my voice hitching despite my best effort at control.

I can't let this happen. Won't let this happen. For a moment, I'm back in Zake's stable, trying to talk him out of hunting a wolf I'd met only in my dreams—needing to try no matter how slim my chances. Twisting my head, I find King Griorgi's eyes, nearly flinching from their familiarity. From the body that is too much like my commander's. "River is losing a great deal of blood. If you truly want him to live, please ask Emperor Jawrar to stop the lashes."

The night guardsman closest to me backhands me across the face, knocking me to the floor. Pain echoes through my body, my face and shoulders stinging. A loud growl rips through the room. Over the reverberating impact, I hear Coal's chains clank as he fights uselessly against them, Tye and

Shade's wolf both lunging for me only to be slammed to the ground by the night guardsmen holding them.

A knife flashes in Griorgi's hand, its point suddenly pressing against the base of my ear. "Stand down, colts," Griorgi tells my males. "Or Emperor Jawrar will have a maimed toy."

The males stop, their breaths ragged. But that little matters just now. Sprawled on the stone, I find River's eyes. They're wild with fury, trained on his father's knife against my neck—fury and fear. My heart aches. I hold his gaze, begging him silently for trust. The kind he's not given me before. The kind that will cost him his pride.

His intelligent gaze pierces mine with confusion. Then, with a twitch of his brow, the male goes slack in his captors' grip. "I'm fine," he growls, the words a perfect, tremulous hair short of being believable. "Worry for yourself, mortal lass."

Smart male. I'm careful not to turn my head as I speak to Griorgi. "You said you wished him to live," I whisper. "Whatever Jawrar's magic is doing, it's not normal. Look."

Griorgi hesitates, glancing at River, whose blood now pools around his knees. However the male manages to increase his own bleeding, I thank the stars for it.

"Jawrar," Griorgi hollers to the qoru. "End the punishment. Dead males learn no lessons."

I catch Shade's golden eyes for a split second then flick them back to Griorgi, praying to all the stars that the wolf gets the message.

I can't see what the emperor does, but whatever has been lashing River stops. The male slumps deeper between the two fae holding him, his breaths fast and shallow, his eyes glazed. Now that the beating has ended, he looks to be on the very edge of consciousness. It's so convincing that even my own throat tightens. Griorgi's eyes widen slightly. The night guardsmen release River's arms and he falls, his face hitting the ground.

In a flash of light, Shade turns to his fae form, holding up his empty hands toward Griorgi. "Will you let me stop the bleeding? He doesn't have too much longer otherwise."

Griorgi's lip curls. Eyes on Shade, he grabs the back of my shirt and hauls me to my feet like a ragdoll. His thick arm wraps around my neck, pressing me against his body. His scent surrounds me, earthy like River's, but with a sour, coppery tang that makes acid rise in my throat. "Move slowly, shifter," he tells Shade. "I'd hate to have to snap this little one's neck for no reason."

Shade draws his hair back into a low, black bun, silently buying me time.

Drawing shallow breaths, I survey the room. Griorgi and Jawrar have ensured that neither we nor Kora's quint can touch each other to summon greater power. Coal and Kora's quint mates are all chained, taking up the last of the restraints. Tye is on his knees. The silver sheen of Shade's magic spiders across River, whose muffled cries of pain draw the hungry gazes of the two qoru soldiers still left. The Night Guard quints are all close enough to each other to form a physical connection if needed. Damn.

Focusing inside me, I catalog what I have. The untamed tiger of Tye's power still simmers in my veins, twining now with the active healing power flowing from Shade. Although I can't touch the male, he's positioned himself as close to me as possible, and I feel him engage all the power he has, shining with it like a small sun. River's magic is the weakest of the three, only a tiny spark from when he made the ground shake earlier.

As for Coal . . . far away and chained . . . I feel nothing from him at all. My gaze cuts to him, finding the male fighting silently against his chains, his blue eyes glazed with fury and panic. Fury and panic that I should be feeling.

Stars, the male is protecting me even now, somehow blocking the feelings to keep me from spiraling in the same horrid darkness that I can see is consuming him. I try to catch his eyes but he refuses to look in my direction, as if doing so would be more than he could bear.

Well, he'll have to get over that, won't he? Because just now, my being different from all the fae is our only hope. I'm weak and small and mortal. And I'm a weaver, the most powerful of beings. I don't need physical contact to connect my quint.

At least, that's my working theory.

Begging the stars that River's pain-filled breaths can keep our captors' attention a bit longer, I force my mind onto a connection of a different sort. During the second trial, Coal was nowhere near me, yet the bridge he built between us worked even with the distance. A bridge that I hope I can build just as well.

Focusing on Coal, I take my mind back to our greatest merging, my thoughts filling with images. Coal's bedchamber. His hands on me. My hands on him. Our connection in a fury of passion and violence, our blood and magic simmering with need.

Coal twitches, his head swiveling in confusion. Yes, he feels it. Feels me.

I press harder. Mercilessly. I fill my mind with the memory of me shoving him atop the bed, driving my nails along his skin until he grabs my wrists. The push and pull of our power, echoing and growing together. My thighs press together even here as the Coal in my mind's eye bends me over the bed. The smell of his arousal—

Coal's cock twitches inside his trousers and the qoru twist toward him.

"It missed us," one says, walking up to Coal. Running a finger along his cheek.

I grip Coal's fierce blue eyes, wishing I didn't have to take him there just now. Not with the qoru who hurt him so close. But we fight with the weapons we have, not the ones we find convenient.

Me. Us. Stay with me, Coal. It is the only way.

Coal grips my eyes. Holds. And after a torturous heartbeat, I feel his answering pang, a bridge made of his own need extending toward me. Power fills my muscles, wakes my nerves, spikes my senses until the cellar seems flooded with light. The magic flows so much stronger than it did over a bridge of nightmares that for a moment I think I could fly.

I force myself back to reality, to the male still holding his arm across my neck. With the cord of Coal's magic joining the others', my body feels full to bursting with power, ready to explode and tear me into shards. I shake as the phantom limbs of magic flail wildly, painfully. My thoughts grow muddled, as if wrapped in cotton.

I have the males' magic but I don't have control of it. The more I struggle to gather the cords together, the more they slip from my grasp. Coal's and Shade's magical strands are the strongest, River's a tiny shadow of what it should be, and Tye's . . . That tiger makes up in power for what it lacks in submission.

"Finish," Griorgi barks at Shade, oblivious to my silent struggle. "Now."

"Sir—" Shade starts to protest.

"River is healed enough to survive the bond break now." Griorgi snaps his fingers at the qoru. "I'm done with the shifter. Feed now, or I'll have him put down."

I slam my elbow into Griorgi's ribs, my hands gripping the arm he has around my neck. With the strength of another world, I yank down on the joint, creating enough space to escape.

"Keep the arm," Coal's voice barks from somewhere in the room.

Arm. Right. One hand sliding over to grip the male's wrist, I ram the heel of my other hand against his elbow.

The king yells in surprise and pain as his joint strains, and he bends to relieve the pressure. Freeing his elbow, Griorgi spins away, turning to face me on slightly bent knees, chest heaving.

Distantly, I notice the night guardsmen preparing to attack and Jawrar stopping them with one hand, a faint smile on his terrifying face. The bastard is curious.

"What the hell are you?" the king demands—a question I'm quickly growing used to. He advances slowly, eyes flashing in a new assessment of me. Larger than River, powerful enough that his mere presence fills the entire room just as his cold gray eyes pierce through me, shattering the bravery I had when I wasn't facing him head-on. Dark, sweaty hair frames Griorgi's severe face, a long scar on it reminding me of another master.

All of a sudden, my breath stutters. My heart leaps into a gallop and blood drains from my face, my hands wet and clumsy. I step back, trip, flail my arms to keep my balance. The magic burbling inside me flares so hard, its aftershocks make the world blink at the edges. Familiar voices shout around me, but I can't work through the words' meanings.

"Answer me, wench," Griorgi booms, his hand rising for a strike. A ring flashes on a large knuckle, its ruby likely to split my face. "What——"

The ground rumbles beneath us, sending both Griorgi and me toppling to the ground. River. A moment of relief floods my body as Griorgi's trance over me dissolves, but then I feel a new sensation.

River's magic, the echo of which has thus far only whispered in my blood, suddenly roars to life. The scent of rocky earth fills my senses, and I can practically feel dry, sandy soil crumbling between my fingers.

The fourth cord.

A final phantom limb of power, fully connecting the quint inside me. If I thought the magic was powerful before, now it's a tsunami that threatens to drown the world. My eardrums ache with the pressure, my scalp tingling as thousands of tiny sparks run up and down my skin. A low keening whistles in my ears, though I can't tell if something is actually making the noise or if it's only in my mind. I grip the strands together—Tye's fire magic, especially, refusing any sort of control. Wild and raw. Indignant as only a feline can get.

Stars, the magic cords have personalities.

I push my way to my knees and blink, the ceiling's wooden beams coming into focus. A dim little candle that somehow made it into the Gloom without its brethren hangs from the center of one rafter. The tiger of Tye's magic roars at the little flame, as if spotting prey that the predator in it can't let pass.

The inferno of power inside me grows, the four cords pulsating with it. Swelling against my grip. Stalking their prey. The magic bunches like living muscle and . . . I feel the power bolting the moment before it happens, my heart freezing with paralyzing, helpless dread.

181

One heartbeat I'm holding the four cords of magic together, and the next they are holding me.

A wordless scream escapes my throat, my body flying back from the force of an explosion. And another. Another. Like Coal's stallion, Czar, who once bolted with me to Mystwood, the strands of the males' magic drag me along with their raging fury.

Flame rises up and up and up, the cracking of wood and stone deafening. I try to let go of the magic, to make it stop, but I can no more halt it than I could stop Czar. The cords wrap themselves tighter around me, pulsing and lashing. Each whip-like strike of power sends a new boom of destruction through the crumbling cellar. The whole top half of the house explodes in a rain of deadly debris. Blue. Red. White. Black.

Shade lunges for me, grabbing my body and rolling to River, who is already throwing up a shield.

"Leralynn!" River's hands are on my cheeks, his beautiful gray eyes filling all of my world.

I struggle to turn, to see what's happening. What I've done.

The stone wall the prisoners were once bolted to no longer exists. Coal, chains still dangling from his limbs, now swings them as weapons to bring down the qoru beside him, blue eyes blazing. Jawrar is nowhere to be seen, having left his qoru and night guardsmen to die for him.

Kora calls an order and the females in her quint pull together, some crawling to make their hands touch. A shimmering green shield springs to life around them, barely in time to stop a blast of splitting stones from crushing them into pulp.

In my side vision, a Night Guard quint closes ranks around the king, moving Griorgi to safety up the shattered stairs just as the world trembles again.

I scream, the cords of power inside me wanting to shatter those stairs to dust. The stairs, the king, the whole world if need be.

"No, look at me," River shouts, shaking me roughly. "Look only at me."

I try. I truly do. My body arches, fear seizing my core. I can't stop the magic. Can't control it. Can't—

"Coal, Tye, connect," River bellows, his hands tightening on my face.

"The king—" I gasp.

"It doesn't matter, Leralynn. Breathe with me. Nothing else matters now." The male's voice turns impossibly calm. "Match my breaths exactly. Do nothing—*nothing*—else. Think of nothing else."

Breathe. I can do that. Focusing on River's chest, I draw a breath. In. Out. In. Out. The flailing cords of power inside me slow, their grip on me loosening. Capitalizing on my small advantage, I snatch at the cords.

They shift.

The ground shakes. Rocks fall, tumbling off River's shield. My lungs seize, every muscle in my body painfully tight.

"Eyes on me, Leralynn," River repeats. "Breathe. I will help you in a moment."

I tremble as Coal and Tye swarm to River, Shade, and me, their hands connecting us together. I feel River's presence at once, a stone pillar in the midst of madness. Like an experienced rider taking a stallion under rein, River gathers the errant power into himself, channeling it safely into the earth below. His body jerks but steadies a heartbeat later as, little by little, he grounds the wild magic.

When my heart slows and my lungs fill with clear, easy breaths, River slides his hands beneath me and lifts me against his chest. "There we go," he says gently. "No more fighting. I don't think Lunos can survive much more of you."

I blink, beholding the crumbled ruins around us. "Did I—"

"I do believe you've got the *powerful* part of being a weaver down pat, lass," Tye says, tugging my hair. "No need to keep proving it, all right?"

"Let's move while there is still a Blaze Court standing," Coal adds darkly and leads the way into the Light.

27

LERA

"So, let me get this straight," Autumn says, scribbling furiously on papers spread around our suite's dining table. "At the end, it was one mortal girl who made the emperor of Mors and king of Slait scamper like cockroaches, leaving their entire conquered town behind?"

"There wasn't much of a town left at that point." Tye spreads himself out on the sunniest part of the couch, his right arm draping over the headrest behind me. "So it wasn't *that* much of a prized possession."

Shade gives me a satisfied grin, the tip of his tongue absently grazing one of his canines. "I feel we should name you something, cub," he says. "Something—"

"That includes the words 'apocalypse' and 'harbinger,'" Coal says darkly. Arms crossed over his chest, the black-clad warrior leans against the wall, taking in everything with his gaze—especially the door.

Having risen first, River went to brief the elders on the situation in Karnish, leaving the rest of us trapped in the suite with Autumn. Denied access to Kora in the infirmary, the petite female has efficiently turned our common room into a cross between a library and interrogation chamber.

Tye's arm drops from the headrest to my waist, and I squeak as he pulls me absently onto his lap. The arm around my waist tightens, keeping me still as tiny prickles of fire magic suddenly dance along my skin—right below the delicate cropped top that Autumn tussled me into.

"If you set Lera's *hand-embroidered* shirt on fire, I will disembowel you," Autumn says, not looking up from her notes.

Tye's fingers flick.

"Bastard!" Autumn jumps up, rubbing a spot behind her ear as she glares at Tye. "You've made me leave a stain."

I bite my lip. Now that I know the amount of skill, training, and control it takes to flick a spark like that, Tye's juvenile pranks have taken on a whole new light. A great many things about Tye have taken on a new light lately. I fidget, yelping as I feel a tiny nip on the top of my ear.

"Stay put, Lilac Girl," Tye says, pressing me firmly back against his soft white tunic. Propping his legs up on the low coffee table, the male rubs his free hand over my neck and arms. "I think you've done quite enough for several lifetimes by now. Plus, you feel good just here and I'd like to enjoy having you in my lap in peace."

"You're insufferable," Autumn mutters.

"Speaking of titles, what do you think we're called now that we've passed the second and third trials but not the first?" Tye says cheerily. "Sparkle, you must have an answer for this, come on."

"Hmm. Maybe 'a pain in my ass'?" Autumn squints at the ceiling. "No, that's your usual state of existence."

I tune them out and glance out the window, the daylight

still disorienting after last night's nightmare. My body aches, though Shade healed my collection of bruises while I was drifting off to sleep last night. I barely recall making our way back through the Gloom, stumbling along until the males insisted on carrying me. "Where do you think Griorgi and Jawrar are now?" I ask, trying not to shiver at the memories.

Autumn bends her head over her notes again and I realize that research is the battlefield she feels most comfortable in. "Slait." She makes a mark, dips her pen into the inkwell, and continues writing. "He is not going to admit that anything is out of the ordinary until he decides to."

I jerk forward. "But he's working with Jawrar—"

"Says who?" The lack of emotion in Autumn's voice makes my chest tighten. The female chews on the tip of her pen, the temperature in the room dropping with each moment of silence. "You? Me? River? You don't go through Slait Court spreading *rumors* about King Griorgi. And you don't attack him unless you are prepared to win."

"So we'll have to prepare for it, won't we?" River says from the doorway.

My whole body tenses, my gaze first surveying the quint commander for marks of last night's injuries—River moves stiffly, but his color seems decent enough—then cutting away from him. Hard. Just looking at the male makes my chest sting with the knowledge of all that he kept from me about his father, his past. Betrayal eats at my lungs like acid.

Autumn's pen drops, her gray eyes tired. "So you are going to do it? Dethrone the bastard?"

River closes a hand around the back of a chair, his face dark. "I don't see that we have much choice. Not now that . . ." He shakes his head. "We'll talk about it tomorrow, when we can all think straight again. Speaking of thinking

187

straight, the infirmary is allowing us to visit Kora's quint after dinner."

My eyes narrow. Dinner first. Then friends. Then, maybe sometime tomorrow, we can get around to discussing how to kill his father. Over lunch. Maybe supper. *Horseshit.*

"It's considered bad form to disembowel a male who's just been whipped," Tye whispers into my ear. "Don't get me wrong, lass, better River than me, but—"

I get to my feet, and this time Tye lets me go without resistance. Coal steps back as I advance on River, Shade flashing prudently into his wolf form and trotting over to curl up on the couch.

River's chin rises. "Leralynn, is something—"

"Your room. Now." I stride past him, catching Tye's murmur of "good luck there, mate" to River before I push open the bedchamber door.

28

LERA

*R*iver winces as he shuts the door behind him, his hands going behind his back. A mask that I want to slap free of his face settles across his features. Calm. Nonchalant. In control.

I take a deep breath. River's room is much like the others', with a large four-poster bed dominating the middle, a wide-open window, and a chest of drawers. He also has a desk and chair, clean sheets of parchment and an inkwell standing at the ready. Familiar, and yet the male's large body, his earthy scent, somehow make the large space suddenly seem small. Intense.

"Leralynn." River's deep voice rolls over me. "What did you wish to discuss?"

"Really, River?" I cross my arms. "You don't know?"

His jaw tightens. He takes a step toward me.

I step back.

He stops. Clears his throat. "I never thanked you, did I? You are the one who saved all our lives last night. If you hadn't interfered when you did, things might have ended differently. Would have ended differently. The courage it must have taken to grab hold of that much power—"

"Wrong answer," I snap. "Try again."

River draws a breath and rolls back his shoulders, the motion making him stiffen in pain. "I'm sorry you were dragged into a problem that my family appears to have started. Thank you for—"

"Try again, River." I raise my chin. "And if you decide to *thank* me one more time for doing what any member of a quint would do for any other, I will walk out this door right now and not speak to you again until you pull your head from your ass."

River's nostrils flare and he crosses his arms in a mirror of mine. Then uncrosses them with a sigh. His neck bobs as he swallows, his cheeks and ears taking on a darker hue. Something in his back shifts, and in that moment, River suddenly looks . . . exposed. Vulnerable enough to make me want to wrap my arms around his neck and pull him against me.

I wait.

"I should have told you about my father," he says quietly. "The whole of it, not just the insinuations. Should have told you that Klarissa was pushing me to take the Slait throne. And why I can't—couldn't. And may have to anyway. I . . . am sorry, Leralynn."

"Better." I walk forward, taking the chair for myself as all the fight goes out of me at once, fatigue taking its place. Plus, with River practically four times my size, there is little point in standing anyway. "Do you want to start with the explanation of what the hell happened with your father, or why you hid it from me?"

"I'd prefer to go into neither," River mutters, the

vulnerable truth of it flashing again in his gray eyes. He walks over to sit on the bed a few paces away from my chair, and this time, when he sits, he lets me see his cringe of pain. "But I imagine I've lost the privilege of keeping secrets, haven't I?"

My neck tightens. "You don't trust me with the truth?"

"What?" He shakes his head, running his hand through his hair. "No, Leralynn. I trust you. I . . . I am not proud of my heritage. And yes, I do worry that you might force me into something behind my back—"

"What—"

"Like, say, a second trial that I haven't approved—but that's not the same."

The last is said with neither condemnation nor apology, and it's my turn to flinch. "All right. I'm too honest to promise that would never happen," I admit.

A small corner of River's mouth twitches. "All right then." He pauses, the humor draining to leave discomfort. "Can I make one request while we talk?" he says hesitantly. "Would you permit me to hold you?"

"Hold me?" I echo.

"It would be easier to speak if I didn't have to toss the words across the room." River shakes his head. "It would be easier to speak if I could feel you against my skin," he says, correcting himself with visible effort. "Please."

I frown, confusion mixing with my fatigue. I little see how the touch of skin would help anything just now. River isn't in love with me, not the way he was with Daz, and it would be better if no illusion of intimacy clouded my senses just now.

His shoulders curl in on themselves.

Sliding off my chair, I decide on a middle ground and pull myself up on the bed beside him. Close, but not touching.

Before I can settle, the large male plucks me up in mid-motion, redirecting me to his lap. His chin rests atop my hair and he sighs, some tension going out of his injured muscles.

"River." I twist to put a hand on his face. *What are you doing? Why?* "You shouldn't be doing this. Not when you are hurt." *Not when you don't mean what you hint at.*

"You weigh nothing, Leralynn," the warrior answers. Then he pauses again, catching his words. "Yes, the lashes hurt. But not very much, and the results were well worth the pain."

I shake myself. Find his eyes. "I don't understand you. In the hours before the trial, you made it rather plain that—"

"I know what I did." River flinches. "You shouldn't have had to lie with a stranger, but I didn't know what else to do. I couldn't bring myself to tell you the truth about my family, but I still wanted to give you all the protection I could and . . . Practicality seemed the best option at the time."

I brush my hand along his strong cheek, the slight prickle of his stubble rasping under my fingers. He is trying. Hard. And my heart breaks for the effort it takes him to voice even these small confessions, though I'm still confused about his feelings. More confused. All right. One step at a time. "Tell me about your father," I order softly. "What happened?"

The words come slowly, River pausing to collect himself as he speaks of his colthood, meeting Klarissa, following her encouragement toward rebellion. The disastrous results that left River and Autumn without a mother and that forever ingrained the nature of the man sitting on Slait's throne in River's mind. River's desire to never, ever, go near the throne again.

"Klarissa wanted to dethrone Griorgi before she ever sent us to Karnish," River says, his body tight around mine, his arms squeezing so hard that it hurts. "She asked me to consider it after the initial word of the attacks on Blaze, knowing my involvement there, as a representative of the Slait throne, would be a direct challenge to my father's power. I said no. You know what happened next. And now I don't think there is a choice in the matter. Not now that Griorgi has allied with Jawrar and found a way to bring qoru into the mainland. We can't let Griorgi break Lunos."

I squirm to get out of River's grip and turn until I'm straddling his lap, my face in line with his. He tries to avert his eyes but I catch his face, turning it toward me. "Is it standing against your father that scares you, River? Or taking the Slait throne?"

"Both," he whispers, his beautiful eyes tight with pain.

"Then we'll do it." I bring my face so close to his that our breath mingles. "Together. All of us."

"Stars." River closes his eyes, a small chuckle escaping his chest. "You've enough fire in your blood to set all of Lunos ablaze."

"Literally," I mutter.

River throws back his head and laughs—a rare sight that's so distractingly stunning, I'm almost relieved it doesn't happen more often. "True. In fact, I just might be holding the most dangerous being in Lunos very close to my rather sensitive areas."

Color rises to my cheeks. I try to turn my face, but River grasps my chin firmly between his thumb and forefinger.

"Your power is a good thing, Leralynn. More than a good thing—a great thing." His voice lowers, all traces of humor gone. "And I am eternally grateful to whatever ancient beings gifted you with it, and gifted our quint with you."

Warmth spreads through me, starting from the spot where

River holds my face and slowly filling my chest. "Even if I occasionally try to destroy the world?"

River smiles, the handsome crags of his face making my lungs tighten. "We'll work on that part."

"I can agree to that." The corners of my mouth tug up.

Before I can get too comfortable where I am, River slides his hands to my arms and pins me in place against him, restraining me for the second time. A habit that should be annoying but is somehow turning my bones to liquid instead. I shift beneath River's attention, drawing a breath when my backside brushes against a sudden hardness.

"While I am offering confessions," River says, his gray eyes flashing, focusing on mine with thunderous intensity. "There is one other lie that I feel the need to correct." Without waiting for a response, River lowers his mouth to mine, his fresh scent drifting around my body in a caress. As one warm palm moves to cup the back of my head, his tongue opens my lips.

I gasp as River claims my mouth, pressing into me so thoroughly that I feel the pounding of his heart echo through my flesh. His tongue dances and twists against mine, marking its territory with a visceral need that leaves no room for doubt of what he wants. Of how much he wants it.

My heart jumps. I press back against River's kiss, the pressure of his lips waking my body, pulling a moan from me before I can stop it. River growls against my mouth, the hand on the back of my head tangling in my hair until I could no more escape his kiss than I could give up breathing.

And stars, I do not want to escape it. Not with my thighs tingling, an ache starting low in my belly. When River pulls away, leaving my lips swollen and empty, my breath hitches from the loss. "What was"—I struggle to remember the start of this conversation—"what was the other lie?"

"When I asked to couple with you," River says quietly. "I said I wanted you for prudence's sake. That wasn't true." He leans down, biting my lip and groaning softly at my gasp of arousal. His hardness presses into me. "I want you because I want you. And I want to prove it."

29

LERA

*M*y breath stops. My underthings are already damp from River's sheer presence. Prove. Prove *it*. Now. Stars. But . . . "But what about Daz?" I blurt, unable to stop either the question or the flash of pain that her name sends through me. I take a breath, struggling to banish the damn stinging in my eyes. "You love her. Not . . . I thought . . ."

River's eyes widen for a moment before something fierce, almost desperate, settles over his features. "You are wrong." The certainty in his voice is hard as steel. Taking my face in his hands, he forces me to look at him even as a single tear I can't stop spills down my cheek. "Leralynn. Listen to me." He takes a deep breath, his broad chest rising and settling again. "I loved Daz. And a part of me will always continue to cherish the time we had together. But she and I, we were never right for each other. Not now and not back all those centuries ago. Until I met you, I didn't know what *right* even felt like. And now I do. I love you, Leralynn."

My breath catches. I stare at him, his words ricocheting around my mind, taking a moment to make sense. River loves me. I feel right to him. I . . . I shift in his lap, my body suddenly needing to be closer to him, even as my mind struggles to catch up.

River shudders as my small motion brushes against his cock, his body's reactions lending weight to his claim. He pulls my face closer to his, nostrils flaring delicately. "Stars, I smell you," he growls. "At least some part of you believes me, then. Before I'm done, I promise that the rest of you shall have no doubts as well."

With a warrior's preternatural speed, River spins me onto the bed, his muscled body looming over me. Reaching behind him, he pulls the shirt off his back and chucks it into a corner. Muscles coil and flex beneath his broad chest, which expands with every hungry breath.

"But . . ." My words fight through the dryness in my mouth. The cuts from Jawrar's invisible whip are barely closed, the tender skin unlikely to be happy with this plan. "You are hurt. This will—"

"Yes, it will," River says, his eyes blazing with need. Intertwining his fingers with mine, he spreads my arms out wide until our bodies are flush. His warm lips graze my ear. "And I can't tell you just how little I care about getting the sheets messy."

River

RIVER'S BODY roared with pain, coming from his back, yes, but mostly from the pressure building so intensely in his balls that he wanted to howl to the skies for release.

But he wouldn't. No, he would keep himself in check however long it took to correct one of the worst damn lies of his life. Before he was through, Leralynn would know—would *believe* in every fiber of her being—just how badly he wanted her.

A shiver pierced River's spine, the intensity of his desire feeling raw to scrutiny. The last time Leralynn had let him into her bed, he had hurt her. Made her feel unwanted while he . . . Stars take him. He'd intended to keep the coupling purely practical, but one look at Leralynn's full breasts, one moment of her wicked tightness around him, and all of River's intentions had burned up in a blaze.

And now it was happening again.

With Leralynn's lilac scent filling his nose, thinking was quickly becoming impossible. But he had to think. He had to figure out a plan before he hurt her again. The girl might not like being taken the way he wished to take her. Intensely. Fully. Her body, her sex, her soul.

River drew in a ragged breath, his cock twitching painfully. Which way to go? Rein himself in hard, or let go completely? Be true or be safe? River teetered on a cliff's edge, no ground in sight.

"What are you thinking?" Leralynn whispered.

"That I'm afraid," River heard himself say. Bracing himself on his arms, he hovered over her, breathing in her intoxicating arousal. Her rich auburn hair spread in shining waves across the pillow, her pale skin flushed with desire, her melted-chocolate eyes showing every thought, every emotion. She hid nothing from him, and he loved her for it. So much it hurt.

River groaned. He'd never let himself go before—certainly not with Daz, and that female had been fae. What if—

"Trust me, River," Leralynn whispered, as if reading his thoughts, her gaze penetrating right through to his soul and stripping it bare. "Show me who you are."

With a roar, River grabbed Leralynn's shirt, ripping the fabric with a single jerk. One more slide of his hand freed her breasts. Grasping both of her wrists in one hand, River stretched her arms over her head, his other hand brushing down her perfect body. Leralynn's full breasts, firm and ripe in his palm, sent a shiver all the way down to his twitching cock.

"You are gorgeous," he whispered, grazing his thumb over a rosy nipple, watching it tighten and spring up like he wanted another part of Leralynn's body to be doing. He dipped his free hand into her loose silk pants, brushing across the curls of her sex. Stars, she was wet already. For him.

Fingers pressed against her moist mound, River took Leralynn's mouth again, hard and deep.

She moaned, rolling her hips to rub against his hand, the scent of her arousal filling River's nose like the wildest of wines. Oh, he wanted more of it. He wanted that scent so heavy that it would fill his room for days to come. And stars, he would tease it out of her body, the throbbing pain in his own cock be damned.

Leralynn's hips came up again, her slickness covering his palm. Her moans of need and frustration only a prelude to what he knew he'd do. Sliding his fingers between her folds, River found Leralynn's opening and thrust one finger deep into her. Hard and fast. Stars, she was tight, and the way her sex closed around his hand . . .

River pulled his mouth away, his eyes flashing when she

tried to protest his hand withdrawing as well. "Stay still," he ordered, sliding his hands along her smooth body, hooking his fingers into the waistband of her loose pants. With a quick motion, he had Leralynn's hips in the air, her pants and underthings sliding off until she was naked for him.

He swallowed a groan at the sight, the perfect flare of her hips and thighs, the glistening curls between them that were the same fiery brown as her hair.

Leralynn whimpered and reached for his neck, her back rising from the bed.

"I said be still." He snapped the words, enjoying watching the female's eyes widen, her hips undulate of their own accord. Yes, she liked his command, even as she disliked liking it. Stars take him, but Leralynn was perfect.

Her breaths ragged, she returned her upper body to the bed, sinking into the soft coverlet.

"Good." Fisting his hand in her hair, River held her as he bent to claim her swollen lips. She melted beneath him, the most cock-hardening moan of pleasure River had ever heard escaping her luscious mouth. He sucked on her bottom lip, enjoying her sweetness, before pulling away to capture her gaze.

Her heart beat so quickly that River could see her pulse vibrating in the soft hollow of her neck. Beneath him, her body trembled with need, the slickness between her thighs shimmering in the light and spilling over the sheets.

River made his voice low. Undeniable in its dominance. "Stretch your hands over your head."

When she did, her potent mix of craving and trepidation saturating the room, River wrapped the silk fabric of her pants around her wrists. Holding her gaze, his attention focused on nothing but Leralynn, River tied the loose ends of the fabric to one of the bedposts.

She tested the restraints. Discovered there was no give. Gasped.

With a soft growl, River lifted her hips, spreading her wide open for his pleasure. More beads of delicious slickness spilled as he set Leralynn's legs on his shoulders and brushed his thumb over her swollen bud.

Leralynn sucked in a breath, bucking so violently that River nearly found his release then and there.

Instead, he hoisted her legs higher on his shoulders and, gripping the insides of her wet thighs, spread her further. He plunged two fingers into her opening this time, in and out, in and out, as his mouth closed around her clit and sucked.

30

LERA

*M*y body jerks, the storm of sensations racing from my sex so strong that my lungs tighten. River's mouth pulls on my bud, each suckle shoving me up a new rung of sensation so fully that I don't realize River's hand is exploring my sex until . . . Two fingers thrust into me, impaling deep and hard. Making me buck, which only pushes my apex deeper into his mouth. Too much. The *thrust, thrust, thrust* of his hand, fast and merciless along my spasming channel, the flaming heat that River's tongue and lips send shooting from my bud.

His mouth still on me, River's wet fingers slide out from my channel and brush along the length of my folds. Up and down, up and—I suck in a startled breath as I feel a slick finger circling my back hole. The pressure growing more insistent with each pass. No. Oh, no no no.

River's tongue flicks against my apex, bringing me painfully close to release. "Relax," he orders, spreading more of my wetness to his new target. Confident. Undeniable. "Take a breath and relax."

The moment I do, a painful stretching fills my backside. I try to tighten but it's much too late. River's finger penetrates the tight ring of muscle and slides in with a bouquet of sensations that magnify everything. A moment later, two other fingers slide right back into my sex. Filling both channels. A new wave of need and pleasure ripples from our connection, gripping me all the way to my curling toes.

I jerk against the restraints, as unyielding as the iron arm holding my thighs open. There is no place to go. No escape. Nothing to do but feel every one of River's merciless strokes that shove me closer to the edge of the abyss. My very lack of freedom somehow fuels my desire, heightening every sensation.

How much I like this makes as little sense as River's words did. His insistence that it's me, not Daz, who he longs for. And yet—yet my body responds to his every touch. The complete attention that River focuses on me is as arousing as his fingers filling my sex . . . and more.

"Stop thinking, Leralynn," he orders, grazing my bud with his teeth to emphasize his point. His voice is even deeper than usual, low and masculine and sex-clenchingly commanding. "Just feel."

My breaths come in gasps, my body struggling despite the futility of it. I tighten my sex as if I can trap River's fingers inside me, keep them a moment longer. When he stops long enough to free himself, I whimper with relief—until I get a good look at that cock of his. Long and wide and already glistening with droplets of him.

I shudder as River lowers my hips and swirls his cock's head in my wetness, his gray eyes meeting mine with predatory intent. He reaches forward to stroke my peaked nipple, then suddenly pinches it hard enough to send a sharp sting from the breast directly to my bud. The sting reaches my sex at the same moment that River buries himself inside me, the tiny pain turning to unbearable pleasure.

He doesn't wait. Gives me no chance to adjust to his great size before his cock finds a target deep inside me, pounding it with forceful strokes that make me clench and moan uncontrollably. The bed creaks with our movement and I pull against my restraints, wishing I could sink my nails into his backside to pull him even deeper. Right when I think I can't take it anymore, River claims my mouth and skims his thumb across my apex at the same time, sending me toppling over the edge with a scream of pleasure.

He shouts with his own release a heartbeat later, panting as he goes limp and falls atop me. With great effort, he finds the strength to rise to his knees and set my hands loose. I run my palms over River's muscles, still trembling with the aftershocks of release. *My male.* Wrapping my arms around his neck, I nuzzle into him, taking in his scent of earth and maleness and climax. Great, powerful, predatory male. *Mine.*

Without thinking, I sink my teeth into the tender juncture of River's neck and shoulder.

The speed with which River awakens, jerking upright with his cock so hard I can see it twitch with every heartbeat, makes me choke on a laugh. Eyes flashing, River flips me onto my belly and takes me again until all thoughts of rebellion are muffled beneath unbearable pleasure.

"Would this be a good time to tell you that the shirt you ripped off me was actually Autumn's?" I say, as River and I finally find the floor, our eyes still glistening with afterglow. His cuts have opened, of course, and he sinks obediently into a chair as I drown a washcloth in a basin atop his dresser.

"I'll make it up to Autumn later," he says between clenched teeth, hissing as I press the cloth to a cut.

I dab gently, though the giant of a male still jumps at each brush of the cloth. "You are a terrible patient," I say, pressing a kiss to the top of his shoulder and receiving a wry look in response. "All right, so you've a plan for Autumn. What about me?"

"I've a plan for that too." River rises, ignoring my protests, and pulls a package out from one of his drawers. "I was saving this until we passed all the trials, but I think today feels appropriate."

Taking the wrapped bundle from River's hands, I tug the strings and open the paper to reveal a gown of golden yellow silk, its skirt made to breathe and flow with the mildest of breezes. My breath halts, my fingers running wonderingly along the fabric. "It's exquisite," I whisper, looking at River. "Like a piece of the sun made real."

Taking the dress from my hands, River slips it over my head, the cool silk falling perfectly over my hips. "You are the sun made real, Leralynn," he whispers into my ear. "The dress is just an accessory."

Excusing myself from River's room to find a fresh pair of underthings and brush the tangles out of my hair, I return to the common room to find Shade's wolf sleeping and Autumn giving me such a knowing look that my cheeks burn.

"I like the dress," she says, her lips quivering to keep a grin in check.

"Mortal." Coal's call seems a welcome escape until I turn to find the penetrating intensity of his eyes. When he crooks a finger to call me over, warning bells clatter in my mind. And here I thought we were done with pre-dinner surprises. As I stride over to him, the smooth honey-gold fabric of my dress caressing my thighs, the male's gaze never leaves mine. Coal steps backward as I approach so we slide into the corridor on his side of the suite, the small step suddenly distancing us from the main-room banter.

Coal crosses corded arms over his chest, leaning one shoulder against the wall. His eyes, stormy in the low light, pierce mine. "What happened during the fight with Griorgi?" he demands quietly.

"I—the magical cords inside me overwhelmed my control." I stumble on the words with a sinking feeling that Coal is asking about something else. That his keen eyes did not miss a single one of my motions in that cellar, no matter that he was chained to a wall.

"You escaped a guillotine hold and attacked the bastard's elbow, and then you froze like a cowering puppy hearing an angry master's footsteps," Coal says bluntly. He takes hold of my chin before I can turn away, his blue eyes preventing even my gaze from escaping. "What happened, mortal? What did you see?"

My muscles tense and Coal's grip tightens, a warning against running before I even start. "It was stupid," I huff, though my heart quickens at the paralyzing memory. Griorgi's large form advancing on me, the sheer powerlessness of the moment, the knowledge of the coming strike. As if I've not faced more serious problems before. "My mind was muddled with the magic and . . . and it won't happen again."

"Yes, it will," Coal says softly. "If you are going to go

rummaging through my nightmares and fears, I'm sure as hell going to rummage through yours. And we'll get out of them together. Now. What did you see?"

"Master Zake," I whisper, heat filling my cheeks. Damn Coal for making me say this. For making me acknowledge it at all. I bite my lip, tasting a bit of blood. "I stand up to the bloody king of Slait, and then he reminds me of a pitiful human and I crumble like sand. It's . . ."

"It's something I understand." Coal leans down, his brilliant blue eyes never leaving mine as he brushes a kiss over my lips. "Not that I'm going to let it lie in ambush inside your mind," he adds, a corner of his mouth twitching to take the sting out of the promise. "But I do understand."

Warmth spreads through me despite the warning, and I lean my head against Coal's hard chest. The *thump, thump, thump* of his steady heart sends waves of safety through me. When Coal's hand slides between my shoulder blades to my lower back, turning me back toward the common room, I twist to look at him over my shoulder. "This is where normal beings would offer a hug. In case you wanted to practice."

"I don't want to practice," Coal informs me. "I do, however, want to keep our common room from being destroyed."

I frown, taking in the space. Everything seems perfectly normal. Autumn stands on her toes to adjust River's shirt collar. Shade's wolf snoozes on the couch, one ear resting on his fuzzy paws. Tye, dressed in black plants and a golden shirt with ruffled cuffs, is striding from his bedchamber. "Is the room in danger?" I ask quietly.

"Watch Tye," Coal murmurs into my ear, starting a slow count. "Ten, nine—"

"What—" That's as far as I get before I realize something

is off with the male's outfit. Golden shirt. Black pants. *One* boot.

The previously sleeping Shade is suddenly up and off the couch, streaking across the floor with speed to rival a sprinting panther.

"I am going to skin you," Tye bellows, his emerald eyes flashing murder as Shade's sleek gray form circles around him at full stride. A dark object in Tye's hand, which I belatedly realize is the gnarled remnant of a chewed-up boot, goes flying at Shade's head.

The wolf fishtails to avoid the boot, knocking Autumn off her feet in the process. The small female falls, curses, and comes to her feet with sparks blazing.

"Zero," Coal finishes behind me and strides into the common room. "Come, mortal, we've a world to save."

The End

∿

Finish the adventure in *Lera of Lunos, Power of Five Book 4.*

Reviews are a book's lifeblood. Please support Lera's story by reviewing this book on Amazon. Just one sentence helps a lot.

ALSO BY ALEX LIDELL

New Adult Fantasy Romance
POWER OF FIVE (Reverse Harem Fantasy)
POWER OF FIVE
MISTAKE OF MAGIC
TRIAL OF THREE
LERA OF LUNOS

Young Adult Fantasy Novels
TIDES
FIRST COMMAND (Prequel Novella)
AIR AND ASH
WAR AND WIND
SEA AND SAND

SCOUT
TRACING SHADOWS
UNRAVELING DARKNESS

TILDOR
THE CADET OF TILDOR

~

SIGN UP FOR NEW RELEASE NOTIFICATIONS at
https://links.alexlidell.com/News

ABOUT THE AUTHOR

Alex Lidell is an Amazon KU All Star Top 50 Author Awards winner (July, 2018). Her debut novel, THE CADET OF TILDOR (Penguin, 2013) was an Amazon Breakout Novel Awards finalist. Her Reverse Harem romances, POWER OF FIVE and MISTAKE OF MAGIC, both received Amazon KU Top 100 awards for individual titles.

Alex is an avid horseback rider, a (bad) hockey player, and an ice-cream addict. Born in Russia, Alex learned English in elementary school, where a thoughtful librarian placed a copy of Tamora Pierce's ALANNA in Alex's hands. In addition to becoming the first English book Alex read for fun, ALANNA started Alex's life long love for fantasy books. Alex lives in Washington, DC.

Join Alex's newsletter for news, bonus content and sneak peeks: https://links.alexlidell.com/News

Find out more on Alex's website: www.alexlidell.com

SIGN UP FOR NEWS AND RELEASE NOTIFICATIONS

Connect with Alex!
www.alexlidell.com
alex@alexlidell.com